序 言

　　在台灣，**英語面談**已經是一種趨勢，無論是求職、留學、移民或升學考試，英文口試幾乎已成為不可或缺的一環。如何以流利的英文，在應對之間充分表達自我，將成為您邁向人生另一個階段前的重大考驗。

　　本書第一篇**求職面面觀**，是針對一般求職者來設計的，內容包含求職面談時，會被問及的所有相關問題。而第二篇**求職實況對話**，則是再細分為八大行業，深入探討面試應答技巧。求職者只要根據自己的情況，充分演練，那麼理想的工作必定手到擒來。

　　第三篇**簽證面面觀**，是針對欲申請簽證者所編寫的。現在，無論您是打算出國留學或移民，只要踏出國門，就必須要申請簽證。欲申請留學簽證者，請參考本書第四篇；而想要辦理移民簽證者，請參考本書第五篇。要申請簽證的讀者，務必要仔細閱讀，並注意回答時的技巧和方向。

　　此外，為了讓「**面談英語**」一書的內容更加完善，本書第六篇還附有撰寫**自傳信函的範例**，第七篇更整理了各類研究所口試中英文常考試題，與相關注意事項。衷心希望能夠提供給讀者最大的效用。

　　本書的編輯，係經多方蒐集最新資料，及審慎的斟酌與校訂之後，方才完成。但仍恐有不足或錯漏之處，誠盼各屆先進不吝指正。

編者　謹識

CONTENTS

第一篇　求職面面觀　Job Hunting English

第二篇　求職實況會話　English Conversation for Job Interview

第三篇　簽證面面觀　Visa English

第四篇　留學簽證實況會話　Interview for Studying Abroad

第五篇　移民簽證實況會話　Interview for Emigration

第六篇　自傳‧信函　Autobiography & Letter

第七篇　補充資料　More Information

☺ 研究所口試相關資料

本書製作過程

　　本書之所以完成，是一個團隊的力量。非
常感謝美籍老師 Laura E. Stewart 和謝靜芳
老師審慎的校閱，白雪嬌小姐負責設計專業的
封面及美編，還要感謝黃淑貞小姐負責版面設
計，以及洪偉華小姐、洪佳穗小姐、鍾明淨小
姐協助整理資料與打字。

第①篇 ▶ 求職面面觀

Job Hunting English

 求職必勝祕技

1. 如何尋找心目中的理想工作

　　許多初出茅廬的社會新鮮人，在踏出職場的第一步時，往往感到非常困惑和緊張，一方面不知道什麼工作才適合自己，另一方面也急著想大展身手，因此，到處投履歷表的結果，往往多是石沉大海，音訊全無。在此，要教諸位讀者如何做好充份的準備，讓您在求職路上無往不利，遠離「畢業即失業」的魔咒。

　　首先，在拿起報紙的求職欄，胡亂打紅圈之前，應該先靜下心來，仔細評估自己的個性、興趣、性向、能力、學歷，並根據這五點來過濾自己想要的工作，或是足以勝任的工作，然後再配合職場所需求的條件，來找出最適合自己的工作。雖然每個求職者都渴望「錢多事少離家近」，不過，對於新鮮人而言，短時間之內是很難找到百分之百滿意的工作，但是有工作總比沒工作好。找工作時，絕對要避免好高騖遠、眼高手低的心態，保持彈性，可以讓您更快適應複雜的職場。

　　當您確定了自己的求職方向後，就可以開始從各個管道著手找工作。最簡單的方法就是從報紙上的求職欄開始，仔細地閱讀，並從中選出讓您感興趣的工作。再來，您可以上求職網站填寫履歷表。在專業的求職網站中，只要您詳細填寫格式化的履歷表，這些網站就會免費幫您媒和，找出適合您的工作，您甚至不需要辛苦地到各個企業投履歷表，只要善加利用這些網站，以電子郵件的方式寄出履歷表，就會有人主動通知您前往面試，這種現代化的求職管道，不但省時省力，也是最有效率的。最後，您還可以動員所有的人際關係，也就是請您的親朋好友，多幫您留意各類的工作機會，千萬別小看人際資源的力量，這也是一條值得一試的求職管道。

以下列出台灣三大求職網站：

1111 人力銀行	http://www.1111.com.tw
104 人力銀行	http://www.104.com.tw
泛亞人力銀行	http://www.9999.com.tw

面對繁複的徵才廣告，想必會令求職者眼花撩亂。不過，此時請務必保持清醒，因爲這可是關係著您一生的前途，絕不能被廣告中的誇大字眼沖昏頭，而誤入歧途。以下，我們將告訴您如何分辨求職陷阱。

第一，在閱讀求職廣告時，請注意以下幾點標示是否清晰，如公司的名稱、地址、電話、所徵求的職務、應徵條件等等。如果內文出現「某大公司誠徵…」、「待遇輕鬆，月入數十萬」、「純內勤，免經驗，可借貸」這類的字眼，且聯絡的電話或公司地址標示不明，請務必加倍小心。畢竟天下沒有白吃的午餐，坐享高薪收入，卻沒有任何的條件限制，絕對不合常理，而且相當可疑。這些徵人廣告有可能是非法的投資公司（如高利貸），或色情行業想拉攏生意的噱頭，切記便宜勿貪，小心因小失大。

第二，你可以向一些職場老手打聽公司的背景（例如：有沒有聽過這家公司？），或是透過政府管道來查詢公司的相關資料，並評估該則徵人廣告的可信度有多高。如經濟部公司登記資料庫（http://www.moea.gov.tw/~doc/ce/cesc1004.html）、和台北市商業管理處（http://ooca.dortp.gov.tw/），這些網站可以查詢該公司是否爲合法登記，且領有事業執照的企業？還有公司的電話地址是否正確？若您還是禁不起廣告的誘惑，想要前往面試，那麼在對方與您聯絡時，務必要仔細詢問，工作內容爲何？公司規模大小等。假如對方支吾其詞、或不願意在電話裡回答，一定要您親自前往面談；或是死纏爛打，甚至在電話裡向您推銷產品，那這家公司一定有問題，絕對不是單純正派的公司企業，求職者千萬不可冒

險應徵。此外，應徵時間請選在一般正常上班時間，最好不要單獨前往，也不要繳交任何保證金或簽約金，相信自己的直覺，假如覺得情況不對，不要猶豫，找個藉口趕快離開，沒找到工作事小，要是被騙財騙色，甚至因而送命，就得不償失了。無論如何，一切以安全至上。

2. 如何填寫履歷表

當您選定求職目標後，一份完善的履歷表就是成功的第一步。怎麼樣才能寫一份吸引人的履歷表，讓雇主看過就產生深刻而良好的印象呢？請把握以下幾個重點：

首先，履歷表就是您給別人的第一印象。所以，越具特色和創意的履歷表，就越能幫助您從成千上萬的應徵者中脫穎而出。寫履歷表時雖不必字字斟酌，文情並茂，但文句流暢，筆跡清楚整齊，則是不可或缺的條件。寫完之後要仔細校正內文，儘量避免出現錯別字，字形字距的大小要拿捏適當，保持版面的乾淨…等，這些都是基本的要求。一份優美整齊、方便閱讀的履歷表，除了賞心悅目之外，還可以傳達給人有誠意、有條理，且細心的好印象。

履歷表的內容，除了寫明應徵公司所要求的基本資料以外（如家庭背景、學經歷），其他的部分（如專長、興趣、理想抱負）應避免平鋪直述，流於單調呆板，要寫出自己的特色。不過，所謂的特色，並不是指標新立異，或捏造不實的內容，而是要表達出個人獨特的風格和品味，讓您的履歷表能獨樹一幟。有特色的履歷表，不但可以加深雇主對您的印象，還可以幫您爭取更多的面試機會。儘量避免使用坊間販賣的制式履歷表，不但了無新意，還會給人一種敷衍了事的感覺。除非公司要求，否則請使用電腦打字排版，這樣看起來既專業又美觀。而照片部分，請按規定使

用最近拍攝的大頭照，千萬不要使用生活照或藝術照（除非您是應徵演員），因為那樣看起來不只是不專業，還會給人輕浮的感覺，所以一定要注意。

在自傳、信函部分，敘述方式應以簡單扼要為主，可以適時添加一點幽默的文采，但不可拖泥帶水，咬文嚼字，過度賣弄文筆，否則可能會引起反效果。假如同時應徵好幾家不同的公司，在填寫履歷表時，就要格外注意每間公司的特殊條件，並配合公司的風格和要求增減修改。但如果所應徵公司之間差異過大，建議最好重新撰寫不同的版本，以免出現牛頭不對馬嘴的情況，而貽笑大方。

3. 面試時的準備

在投出精心撰寫的履歷表之後，經歷漫長的等待而得到回音，想必是十分令人雀躍的事。不過別忘了，我們的最終目的是要被錄取，獲得這份工作。因此，面試的準備更是決定求職成功與否的重大關鍵。

第一個要注意的是——外貌衣著，面試官大多會以第一眼的印象來決定是否錄取此人。所以，如何借助服裝打扮，將自己最完美的一面呈現出來，是個非常重要的步驟。

首先是服裝的搭配，整齊乾淨是基本條件。再來，要試著搭配所應徵的工作與本身的氣質。例如，穿著名牌套裝去應徵業務助理，會給人不協調的感覺，甚至有喧賓奪主的感覺，相當不恰當。若是應徵秘書或設計師，則可以穿著色調柔和，樣式簡單大方的套裝，這樣可以給人穩重專業的印象。男士嚴禁穿著拖鞋、涼鞋、背心或短褲，女士則不宜穿著太曝露的迷你裙，或低胸露背的上衣，也不要濃妝豔抹。另外，過於濃郁的香水，誇張的髮

型、髮色、指甲油…等，也都應該儘量避免。最好以清爽自然、專業大方的打扮為主，不但可以給雇主好感，也可以緩和自己緊張的情緒，否則要是讓面試官一直盯著您的奇裝異服，或是因為您的香水味而猛打噴嚏，都會對面試的結果產生負面影響。

另外，要注意基本的穿著美學。像是較胖的人，要避免穿橫條紋，或過於寬鬆的衣物；皮膚黑的人，不要穿得太暗，以免看起來沒精神。此外，面試之前一定要注意自己的身體清潔，口氣、體味會不會太重？頭髮是否清洗乾淨，吹燙整齊？肩膀上有無頭皮屑？髮膠使用是否過量？男性要記得刮鬍子、修剪鼻毛。女性若穿著短袖或裙子，要記得修剪腋毛和腿毛，絲襪不可有破洞，並注意內衣肩帶是否露出，可上淡妝，以示禮貌，但補妝時要記得到化妝室去，切忌在大庭廣眾下補妝。

在等待面試時，坐立難安是難免的，可是千萬不要焦急地來回踱步，或是咬手指、抽煙、嚼口香糖等。如果真的很緊張，不妨多做幾個深呼吸，來使自己保持沉穩。或者，可以欣賞會客室裡的擺飾或窗外風景。如果同時有其他的應徵者在場，且情況許可的話，可以小聲交談，藉此交流資訊，並舒緩緊張的氣氛，但切勿高聲談笑。面對公司裡的其他人，要表達您的善意，並適時的問候和微笑，畢竟將來有可能會成為同事，可是不能妨礙別人工作，無意義的搭訕或閒談可能會招致反感。

在面談時，要特別注意小細節，像是避免在面試官前抖腳，手機一定要關機等。談吐、應對務必要從容大方，保持耐心，集中注意力聆聽面試官的問題，回答時要掌握重點，簡短扼要，多使用肯定的字眼，避免使用不確定或含糊的字句。另外，不可捏造事實，或批評過去的公司，更不要當面反駁面試官。只要注意到這些細節，相信您的錄取機率必定會倍增。

1 Introduction 介 紹

面試者： Name and examination number, please.
請問你的名字和應試號碼。

應徵者： Number 20. My name is Wang Chih Ming.
我是 20 號，王志明。

面試者： Tell me a little more about yourself, please.
請多告訴我一點關於你自己的事。

應徵者： My name is Wang Chih Ming and I live in Taipei.
I was born in 1982. I am a student at Chengchi
University. I am majoring in public administration.
I like traveling very much and enjoy sports. I am
in the tennis club at my university.
我叫王志明，住在台北，生於 1982 年。我唸政大，主修
公共行政。我非常喜歡旅行，也喜愛運動，大學參加網
球社。

My name is Chen Tzu Yun. I come from Tainan.
I graduated from the political department of National
Taiwan University last year. I like reading, writing
and swimming. I'm a creative and energetic person.
我叫陳詩雲。我來自台南。去年從台大政治系畢業，我
喜歡閱讀、寫作和游泳。我是一個有創造力且精力充沛
的人。

② *Personal History* 個人經歷

面試者：When were you born? 你什麼時候出生的？

應徵者：July 25, 1982. 1982 年 7 月 25 日。

面試者：What's your present address?
你現在住在哪裡？

應徵者：100, Ren-ai Road, Section 1, Taipei.
台北市仁愛路一段 100 號。

面試者：Have you moved often?
你常常搬家嗎？

應徵者：Yes, my family has moved twice. I lived in Tainan
during elementary school and junior high school
and then in my second year of high school we
moved to Taichung, and we moved again to Taipei
when I started college. I've been there ever since.
是的，我搬過兩次家。我小學和國中時都住在台南，高
二搬到台中，開始上大學時又搬到台北，從此就住在那
裡。

No, my parents moved to Taipei thirty years ago.
I was born in Taipei and live in the same place
for twenty-two years.
不，我爸媽三十年前就搬到台北來。我在台北出生，而
且在同一個地方住了二十二年。

面試者： Then when your family moved you had to change high schools? 邢你搬家時，是不是就得轉學？

應徵者： That's right. I transferred from a high school in Tainan to one in Taichung.
是的，我從台南的一所中學轉到台中。

面試者： Did you find it easy to adjust to a new school?
你覺得自己很容易適應新學校嗎？

應徵者： Well, at first everything was so different, and I felt a little strange, but I made a lot of new friends and then it didn't seem strange anymore.
嗯，剛開始每件事都很不一樣，而且我覺得有點陌生，但在我交了很多新朋友之後，好像就不再感到陌生了。

面試者： What school did you graduate from?
你是什麼學校畢業的？

應徵者： I graduated from National Sun Yat-sen University.
我畢業於國立中山大學。

面試者： Have you kept in contact with any of your friends from grade school?
你有沒有和任何小學同學保持聯絡？

應徵者： Yes, it just so happens that one of my friends from grade school is in my university, so whenever we see each other we talk about old friends.
有，正好有一個小學同學和我上同一所大學，所以每當我們兩個見面時，就會談起老朋友。

面試者： What schools have you attended?

你唸過什麼學校？

應徵者： I finished Chung-I Primary School in 1993, and entered Dah Tung Junior High School that same September. I graduated from there in July of 1996 and entered Cheng Kung High School in September of that year. I graduated in July of 1999, and that September I entered Chengchi University, where I'm studying now.

一九九三年，我從忠義國小畢業，同年九月進入大同國中就讀；一九九六年七月國中畢業，同年九月上成功中學；一九九九年七月畢業，同年九月進入政治大學就讀，也就是我現在唸的學校。

面試者： Tell me something about your experiences in high school. 告訴我一些你在高中的經歷。

應徵者： (*smile*) I was in the fencing club, so the first thing comes to my mind is those long, hard practices! I was captain of the club for one year, and that was a really good experience, I think, trying to make the club better and stronger. I learned a lot from that.

（微笑）我參加劍道社，所以我最先想到的就是那些漫長而辛苦的練習！我當了一年的社長，我認為那實在是個很好的經驗，我很努力想使這個社團更好、更茁壯，也從中學到很多東西。

面試者： Did you engage in any clubs in college?
你大學時曾參加過任何社團嗎？

應徵者： Yes, I was a member of the baseball team. We always practiced twice a week. Sometimes we played friendly games with teams from other schools or colleges. What I gained from being on the team is that now I'm better at cooperating with others.
是的，我曾是棒球隊的成員。我們一向是一星期練習兩次。有時我們會和來自其他學校或學院的球隊打友誼賽。參加棒球隊的收穫在於，我現在更擅長與他人合作。

面試者： Your application form says you were out of school for half a year during high school. Why was that? Were you ill?
你的履歷表上說，你高中的時候有半年離開學校，那是為什麼？你生病了嗎？

應徵者： Oh, no. My father's job took him to America for six months, and he decided to take the whole family along.
喔，不是。我父親的工作需要他去美國六個月，他決定帶全家人一起去。

面試者： So during that time you went to high school in the United States? 所以你那時候就在美國唸高中？

應徵者： Yes, it was just for few months, but I attended Hollywood High School in Los Angeles.
是的，雖然只有幾個月，但是我在洛杉磯上好萊塢中學。

面試者： There was a year between the time you graduated from high school and when you entered the university. What were you doing during that time?

在你高中畢業和進大學之間有一年，那段時間你在做什麼？

應徵者： I didn't do well on my first try in the JCEE, so I attended a prep school and studied for a year. Fortunately, I got excellent grades on my second try. Now I'm a senior of NTU.

我第一次考大學時沒考好，所以我進了一家補習班唸了一年的書。很幸運地，我第二次考得很好。現在我是台大四年級學生。

I took some time to do the things a person doesn't usually have time for. Mostly, I traveled.

我花了一些時間去做一般人通常沒有時間做的事，大多是去旅行。

③ Student Life 學生生活

面試者： Was there any teacher who impressed you very deeply?

有沒有哪位老師給你很深刻的印象？

應徵者： Yes, in high school I had a teacher named Mr. Wu. He introduced me to John Irving's books, "The Hotel News Hampshire" and "The Cider House Rules." These two books made a powerful impression on me.

有，在高中的時候，有一位吳老師。他把約翰・厄文的書介紹給我，像「新罕布夏旅館」和「心塵往事」，而這兩本書給我非常深刻的印象。

Yes, when I was in junior high school, my Chinese literature teacher, Miss Chen gave me a rather deep impression. She spent a lot of time with my class. She always said that practice makes perfect, so she gave us many simulated tests. Finally, we really got outstanding grades in this subject.

有，當我還是個國中生時，我的國文老師，陳老師，給我非常深刻的印象。她花了很多時間來陪我們班。她總是說：「熟能生巧」，所以她讓我們考了很多模擬考試。最後，我們果真在這個科目拿到十分出色的成績。

面試者：When you were a student, was there anything you got really seriously involved in?
你當學生時，有沒有真正認真參與過什麼事？

應徵者：Yes, I decided that the best time to travel was while I was a student, so I worked my way around the country during vacations, doing part-time jobs here and there. I met all sorts of different people and it was really a good experience. Of course, there were good parts and bad parts, but looking back I think it did a lot for me. It changed me a lot and helped me grow up.
有，我認為學生時代是旅行的最佳時機，所以放假時我在國內各地工讀，到處兼差。我認識各式各樣的人，那真是很好的經驗。當然，這樣有好有壞，但是回想起來，這對我的幫助很大。它使我改變很多，並幫助我成長。

Well, I joined the judo club when I was a freshman in college, and during the four years I guess I spent more time and energy on judo than on anything else. The practices were really hard, and I don't know how many times I thought about quitting. But looking back on it, the memories are all good. During the practices I'd think, "why am I doing this?" but afterwards I felt really good. I made a lot of friends that way, too, through the club activities.
嗯，我在大一時加入柔道社，我想四年來，我花在柔道社的時間與精力，比任何其他事情多。練習真的很辛苦，而且不曉得有多少次想放棄，但是回想起來，這些回憶都是好的。練習的時候我會想：「我為什麼要這麼辛苦？」但是後來感覺就好多了。經由社團活動，我還交了很多朋友。

面試者 ： What was your favorite subject?
你最喜愛的科目是什麼？

應徵者 ： World history. I liked learning about how the world was changing before I was born. And I'm interested in the recent history of the countries of the world today. It helps me understand the news better, too, if I know some of the background of the Mideast situation, or Africa or Europe.
世界史。我想知道在我出生以前，世界是怎麼變化的。而且我對今日世界各國的近代歷史很有興趣。如果我能知道一些中東局勢，或非洲、歐洲的背景，也有助於我更加了解新聞。

Mathematics. I like geometry especially. I've liked math ever since high school, and then in college I had an excellent teacher. His class was always interesting, and that made me like math even more.
數學。我特別喜歡幾何。從高中起，我就喜歡數學，而且後來在大學時，也碰到一位很好的老師。他的課總是很有趣，那使我更加喜歡數學。

面試者 ： What was your worst subject?
你最差的科目是什麼？

應徵者 ： Mm, that would be chemistry. I never did like it, and my marks weren't ever very good. The chemical formulas were hard for me to understand, and (*smile*) in chemistry class there are always a lot of chemical formulas!
嗯，那就是化學了。我從來沒有真正喜歡過它，所以我的成績也從來沒好過。化學公式對我來說很難理解，而且（微笑）化學課總是有一大堆化學公式！

應徵者： Well, in college you get to choose your own major and other courses, so there was nothing particular that I disliked. But in high school I was terrible at Chinese literature. My mind isn't very liberal arts-oriented, I guess.

嗯，在大學，你必須選自己的主修科目和其他課程，所以我沒有特別討厭的科目。但我高中時的國文卻很糟糕。我想我不大適合唸文科。

面試者： Is there anything you regret not doing or would like to have done differently during college？

你在大學的時候，有沒有什麼是你後悔沒做的，或是想以不同的方式來處理的事？

應徵者： I spent a lot of time on my studies, and got a good, solid grounding in my major area, and that was good, I think. But I think probably it would have been good if I had gotten a little more involved in club activities.

我花了很多時間唸書，並在主修的領域中，奠定了良好而紮實的基礎，我認為那樣很好。但是我想，如果我能多參與一點社團活動，或許也是好的。

I spent a lot of time on club activities and my part-time job during the four years, I didn't fail any of my classes, but looking back on it, I think it would have been better to put more time and energy into studying.

四年當中，我花了很多時間在社團活動和打工上面，我沒有任何一科被當，但是回想起來，如果我多投注一點時間和精力來唸書，那會更好。

4 Family 家 庭

面試者： Where is your family from? 府上哪裡？

應徵者： We're from Pingtung County. 我們是屏東縣人。

面試者： How many are there in your family? (How big is your family?) 你家有幾個人？

應徵者： There are four of us, including me.
包括我有四個人。

There are five people in my family.
我們家有五個人。

面試者： Do you spend much time talking with your family?
你花很多時間和你的家人交談嗎？

應徵者： Oh, yes. People say there's a generation gap in the world today, but I don't think there is one at our house. We all make a point of taking time to talk with each other. Especially at mealtimes, we all get together to eat and talk. Meals are very lively at our house.
喔，是的。聽說今天這個世界是存有代溝的，但是我不認為我們家有代溝。我們都努力花時間和彼此交談。尤其是用餐的時候，我們會聚在一起吃飯和談話，我們家吃飯時是很熱鬧的。

應徵者： Not really. I moved to Taipei four years ago, because it was convenient for me to get to school. My families lives in Kaohsiung, and I always go home once every two months. Though I don't have much time to spend with them, I do cherish every moment we have.

實際上沒有。我搬到台北四年了，因為這樣上學會比較方便。我的家人都住在高雄，我一向都是兩個月回去一次。雖然我沒有花很多時間來陪他們，但我十分珍惜我們所擁有的每一刻。

面試者： Your application form says that you have a younger brother. How do you and he get along?

你的履歷表上說，你有一個弟弟，你和他處得怎麼樣？

應徵者： We get along very well. He's studying for the college entrance exam right now, so he asks me for advice a lot on how he should study and things like that. We go swimming together a lot, and mountain climbing. Of course, we fight sometimes, too, but mostly we get along very well.

我們處得很好。他現在正在準備大學入學考試，所以，他要我給他很多關於怎麼唸書和像這一類的建議，我們常常一起去游泳和爬山。當然，我們有時候也會吵架，但是大部分的時候，我們都處得很好。

⑤ *Character* 個 性

面試者 ： Are you more of a follower or a leader?
你比較像跟隨者，還是領導者？

應徵者 ： I don't try to get in front of people and lead them, particularly. I'd rather cooperate with everybody else, and get the job done by working together.
我不會試圖領先別人，特別是去領導他們。我寧願和其他每一個人合作，並且一起努力完成工作。

In most cases, I'm the leader of my classmates. They always think that I'm a reliable and alert person. And I usually try my best to help them.
在大多數的情況下，我都是擔任我同學的領導者。他們總認為我是個值得信賴，且機靈的人。而我通常也會盡力協助他們。

I don't agree with someone else's opinion if I think he's wrong, but if when I understand what he's thinking and see he has some good ideas, then I'm very happy to go along with him.
如果我認為某人的看法是錯誤的，我就不會贊同他，但是如果我了解他的想法，並且知道他有一些好主意，那麼我會很高興地贊同他的意見。

面試者： What kind of personality do you think you have?
你認為你是什麼樣的人？

應徵者： Well, I approach things very enthusiastically, I think, and I don't like to leave something half done. It makes me nervous —— I can't concentrate on something else until the first thing is finished.
嗯，我想我做事非常熱心，而且我不喜歡做事做一半。那會讓我緊張 —— 除非第一件事做完，否則我無法專心做別的事。

Mm, I'm a creative person. Even if the situation is very urgent or confused, I can still come up with good ideas to solve the problem.
嗯，我是個有創意的人。即使情況十分危急或混亂，我還是可以想出好點子來解決問題。

面試者： Would you describe yourself as outgoing or more reserved? 你覺得自己是外向的，還是比較內向的？

應徵者： Well, I'm not very outgoing, but if I have to make others understand my idea, then I won't be a shy person.
嗯，我不是很外向，但是如果我必須讓別人了解我的想法，那麼我將不會是個害羞的人。

I'm not really sure — maybe partly both. In class, if I had a question I would always go to the teacher and ask, but around my friends I'm pretty quiet.
我不是很確定——也許兩者兼具。在課堂上時，如果我有問題，我總是會去請教老師，但在朋友之間，我非常安靜。

面試者：Do you think you are more outward looking or more inward looking?

你認為你比較外向，還是比較外向？

應徵者：Well, sometimes I want to be by myself, but most of the time I prefer being with a group of people, so I guess you'd say rather outward looking. I was very active in my university club.

嗯，我有時候會想要獨自一個人，但是大部分的時候，我比較喜歡和一群人在一起，所以我想你會說我相當外向。我在大學的社團裡非常活躍。

I like being around people and doing things with people, so outward looking, I guess.

我喜歡待在人群裡，並和別人一起做事，所以我想我是外向的。

面試者：What would you say are some of your faults and strong points?

你說你有哪些缺點和優點？

應徵者：People say that I tend to do a thankless task. I can take on jobs that bother other people and just work at them slowly until they get done. I enjoy that kind of achievement—that's a good point, I suppose. But the reverse of that is I tend to be withdrawn. I need to go out and be with other people more, so I'm working on that.

別人說我很容易去做不划算的事。我能承擔別人感到煩惱的工作，然後慢慢努力，直到把工作完成為止。我喜歡那種成就感—我想那是個優點。但是與此相反的是，我很容易退縮。我必須多出去和別人相處，所以我正在努力改進中。

Well, I'm afraid I'm a poor talker, and that isn't very good, so I've been studying how to speak in public. I suppose a strong point is that I like developing new things and ideas.

嗯，我恐怕不是個會說話的人，而且那不是件好事，所以我一直在學習如何當眾發言。我想我有一個優點，那就是我喜歡開發新的東西和想法。

I think my fault is that I don't like to work on holiday. I believe that without enough rest, people can't do their best. And my strong point is that I'm good at designing projects. As long as you tell me the goal, I can accomplish it.

我覺得我的缺點是，我不喜歡在假日工作。我相信沒有充分的休息，就無法有最佳的表現。而我的優點是，我很擅長專案設計。你只要告訴我目標，我就可以完成它。

⑥ *Friendships* 交 友

面試者： Do you have any people you'd call really close friends?

你有沒有任何真正稱得上親密的朋友？

應徵者： Three people, but two of them live quite away and we only get to see each other every two or three weeks. The other fellow helped me through a bad time when I was a freshman, and we've been close friends ever since.

有三個，但是其中兩個住得很遠，我們每隔兩三個禮拜才見一次面。另外一個在我大一的時候，幫我渡過了一段難熬的日子，從此我們就一直是很親密的朋友。

面試者： Would you say you have a lot of friends, or just a few?

你認為你有很多朋友，還是只有一些？

應徵者： I would say that I have a lot of friends. Some of them were my college classmates, and others were my coworkers at my part-time job. We often needed to cooperate with each other before, so we became really close friends. Now we go out about twice a week, and we always have a good time when we get together.

我會說我有很多朋友。他們有些是我的大學同學,而其他則是我打工時的同事。我們以前常需要一起合作,所以就變成非常親密的朋友。現在我們一個星期大概會出去兩次,而且我們相聚時總是非常愉快。

Not so many, but not really just a few, either, I suppose. There are about six people that I see quite a bit of now. They're good friends.

我想不是很多,但也不是只有一些。我現在經常見面的大概有六個。他們都是好朋友。

7 Interests and Hobbies 興趣與嗜好

面試者： What kind of hobbies do you have?
你有哪方面的嗜好？

應徵者： I like reading and playing the piano.
我喜歡看書和彈鋼琴。

I enjoy sports, and I like music very much.
我喜歡運動，而且非常喜歡音樂。

面試者： What kind of sports do you like? And do you watch,
or play? 你喜歡哪種運動？你是看，還是玩？

應徵者： I like watching and playing both. And I enjoy almost
all sports, but I especially like tennis and gymnastics.
I was in the gymnastics club all through high school,
so particularly in the case of gymnastics I prefer
doing to watching.
我看和玩兩種都喜歡。而且幾乎所有的運動我都喜歡，
但是我特別喜歡網球和體操。整個高中時期我都待在體
操社，所以單單就體操來說，我比較喜歡做，不喜歡看。

I like baseball best. I usually like to practice with
my friends. But when there are big games like the
Asian Championship, I prefer to watch and shout
with my family.
我最喜歡棒球。我通常都喜歡和朋友一起練習。但當有
大型比賽，像亞洲錦標賽時，我就比較喜歡和家人一起
觀賞和尖叫。

面試者：　Do you smoke?　你抽煙嗎？

應徵者：　Yes, I do.　是，我抽煙。

I like drinking, but I don't smoke.
我喜歡喝酒，但是不抽煙。

面試者：　How do you spend your free time?
你怎麼度過你的空閒時間？

應徵者：　I run or play tennis or do something else like that
to get some exercise and keep in shape.
我跑步、打網球，或是做一些別的運動來保持健康。

I play the flute with a group of friends in Tien-mu
Sometimes — we're all amateurs — so I go and
see them every so often.
我有時候會和天母的一群朋友一起吹笛子——我們都是業餘
的，所以我時常去看他們。

I usually watch TV or movies. Also I enjoy surfing
on the Internet and reading e-mail from my friends.
When I bump into old friends on Yahoo Messenger,
we always chat for a long time.
我通常會看電視或看電影。另外，我也喜歡上網和閱讀
朋友寄來的電子郵件。當我在雅虎的即時通訊上碰到老
朋友時，我們總會聊很久。

8 *Books and Authors You Like* 喜歡的書和作家

面試者： What kind of books do you like?
你喜歡哪一類的書？

應徵者： I like mysteries very much — I like to try to figure out "who did it" before the author explains everything. My favorite character is Hercule Poirot in the Agatha Christie mysteries. I've read all of those.
我非常喜歡偵探小說——我喜歡在作者解釋每一件事之前，先試著去找出「是誰做的」。我最喜歡的角色是阿嘉莎‧克莉斯蒂偵探小說裡的赫邱里‧白羅，那些小說我全都讀過了。

I like to read magazines. Because I can learn a lot from that.
我喜歡看雜誌。因為可以從裡面學到很多東西。

I like biographies. It's interesting to read about the backgrounds of people who have become famous and see what I can learn from their lives.
我喜歡傳記。閱讀已成名者的經歷，並看看我能從他們的人生中學到些什麼，是很有意思的。

面試者： Who is your favorite author?

你最喜歡的作家是誰？

應徵者： I like the novels of Hermann Hesse very much.
I've read almost all of them in English translation.
I wish I could read them in the original — I hear
they're even better.

我非常喜歡赫曼赫塞的小說，我幾乎讀了所有的英譯
本，我希望能讀原著──聽說那寫得更好。

My favorite author is Marakami Haruki. I think
he is a very creative writer. He always describes
things in a subtle and humorous way. I've enjoyed
every book he has written.

我最喜歡的作家是村上春樹。我覺得他是個非常有創
意的作家。他總是以細膩而幽默的方式來描寫事物。
我讀過他所寫的每一本書。

面試者： What is the most impressive book you've read
recently?

你最近讀的書裡面，印象最深刻的是哪一本？

應徵者： I read the book " Il Barone ", which was written
by an Italian author, Italo Calvino. It was about
a man who have lived in trees since he was twelve
years old. This book really impressed me with
its interesting and singular plot.

我讀了一本叫做「樹上的男爵」的書，它是由義大利作家伊塔羅·卡爾維諾所寫的。它是描述一個男人的故事，這個男人從十二歲開始就住在樹上。這本書有趣而奇特的情節，令我印象非常深刻。

I read the book that the movie "The Deer Hunter" was based on, about the war in Vietnam, and it made a very deep impression on me. It was the first thing I'd ever read that made war seem real to me. It was quite a shock.

我讀了電影「越戰獵鹿人」的原著小說，那是關於越戰的書，它使我印象非常深刻。這是我第一次讀到讓我眞正感受到戰爭的書，那令我十分震撼。

面試者： What was it that shocked you?

使你感到震撼的是什麼？

應徵者： I guess the tragedy of the fighting and the close friendship that it created among the men. Fighting and friendship always seemed contradictory to me, and that book shows them as very closely related. It's given me a lot to think about.

我想是戰爭的悲劇，和它帶給人們的親密友誼。戰爭和友情對我來說，似乎總是矛盾的，而這本書卻以密切關連的方式來呈現他們。它給了我很多可以思考的東西。

⑨ People You Respect　你尊敬的人

面試者： Can you name one person that you respect very much?　你能不能說出一個你非常尊敬的人？

應徵者： My English teacher in college. She had so much humor and vitality, and I was very impressed with her tactfulness. She could make a person see the contradictions in his thinking without making him feel foolish. I learned a lot from watching the way she applied herself to her teaching, and how she led people to see things.

我大學的英文老師。她非常幽默而且活力十足，她的機智使我留下非常深刻的印象。她能讓一個人知道自己思想上的矛盾，而不讓他覺得自己很蠢。我從她專心教學，引導人們了解事情的方法中，學到很多。

My father. I was born into a middle-class family. My father is a construction worker. Although he has a Bachelor of Architecture degree, he hasn't had a chance to display his ability. He has worked very hard all his life, but he never complains about that. I think he really loves his family and is willing to contribute everything he has to it.

我父親。我出生在一個中產階級的家庭。我父親是一個建築工人。雖然他是個建築學學士，但卻從來沒有機會展現自己的能力。他一輩子都在辛勤工作，可是他從來不抱怨。我想他非常愛他的家庭，而且願意貢獻出他所擁有的一切。

應徵者： Mmm…Dr. Martin Luther King. He impressed me as a man with a great deal of love for mankind with the way he worked for Black liberation and equality. His "I Have a Dream" speech has had a big effect on me. I've listened to that tape hundreds of times.

嗯…是馬丁路德‧金恩博士。他最讓我印象深刻的是，他對人類有豐富的愛心，和他致力於解放黑人與爭取平等的方式。他的演講──「我有一個夢」──對我有很大的影響。那捲錄音帶我已經聽了好幾百遍了。

⑩ *Life Attitude* 生活態度

面試者： What basic principles do you apply to your life?
你應用在生活上的基本原則是什麼？

應徵者： I try to keep to a regular schedule every day. When I don't, my body isn't in good shape, and neither is my mind, so I've been keeping to a schedule ever since I started college.
我每天努力保持規律的作息，如果不這樣，我的身體就會不健康，精神也不好，所以自從我上大學之後，就一直維持固定的作息時間。

I try to keep a child's outlook on some things. I want to continue to see the beauty in flowers and plants and animals — I don't want to lose that.
我試著在看待一些事物時，保有赤子之心。我想繼續欣賞花卉、植物、與動物之美——我不願失去它。

面試者： What's your motto? 你的座右銘是什麼？

應徵者： Never put off till tomorrow what you can do today. I've found out that time and money slip away very easily —— you think you have them, and they're gone! Putting things off just makes it worse later, so even if it's hard at the time, I try to get things done that day and not let them go.

今日事今日畢。我發現時間和金錢非常容易消逝——你以
為你擁有它們，而它們卻不見了！拖延只會使事情後來
變得更糟，所以即使在當時要完成工作是很困難的，我還
是會設法在當天完成，而不會放下工作。

Pardon is the most glorious revenge. I've found
that if I always try to retaliate against people who
treat me badly, I'll become a vindictive person, and
lead an unhappy life. Therefore, now I try to
understand those people and see if we can be friends.
寬恕是最好的報復。我發現，如果我老是試圖報復那些
對我不好的人，我將變成一個復仇心強烈的人，而且會
過著不快樂的生活。因此，我現在會試著去了解那些人，
並看看我們能不能成為朋友。

11 *Ambitions and Aspirations* 抱負與希望

面試者： What made you choose this company?
是什麼原因使你選擇這家公司？

應徵者： I've been interested in computers ever since junior high school. I read every book I could find, and even built a simple computer myself. Your company is the biggest computer company in the world, and I want a chance to apply what I've learned so far, working for you.
我從國中開始就一直對電腦有興趣。我讀我所能找到的每一本書，甚至替自己組了一部簡單的電腦。貴公司是世界上最大的電腦公司，我想要有可以學以致用和為你們工作的機會。

面試者： Tell me why you are interested in working for this company. 告訴我你為什麼想在我們公司工作？

應徵者： I think working in this company would give me the best opportunity to use what I've learned in college, where I studied trade for four years. I think there's a very good future in precision instruments, and they are one of this country's major exports, so for a long time I've been thinking I'd like to work for this company.
我認為在這家公司工作，會給我一個最好的機會，來運用我在大學所學到的東西，我學了四年的貿易。我認為精密儀器的遠景十分看好，而那正是本國主要的外銷品之一，所以我長久以來都一直希望能為這家公司工作。

應徵者：Mr. Lee in the Export Department of your company is from my university. He and I were in the same club together — he was a junior when I was a freshman — and we've kept in touch since then. He told me about his job here and I liked the way the company sounded. He told me that a person advances in your company on his own merits, not depending on his seniority.

貴公司出口部的李先生和我是同一所大學畢業的，他和我一起參加同一個社團 —— 我大一的時候他大三 —— 從那時起，我們就一直保持聯絡。他告訴我他在這裡的工作，而我覺得這家公司聽起來不錯。他告訴我貴公司的升遷是靠自己的表現，而不是看年資。

面試者：What was it that made you decide to choose this company?

是什麼原因使你決定選擇這家公司？

應徵者：Well, I was thinking that I'd like a job somewhere where I could use my English, and then I saw your company's advertisement. It looked really interesting. I think this company has a great future and I'll be able to develop my abilities here. That's why I applied.

嗯，我想說，我要找一個可以運用我的英文能力的工作，然後我看到貴公司的廣告。它看起來真的很有趣。我想這家公司非常有前途，而且我將能在這裡培養自己的能力。這就是我來應徵的原因。

應徵者： Well, in some companies no matter how much ability you have, if you're young, you don't get much responsibility. But people say that in this company, if you can do the job, people will trust you with even important work. That's challenging, I think. Also, I have a friend working here already, so I know a little about the company. Moreover, I'm very interested in cars, and I enjoy developing new designs, so I think I could do good work for you.

嗯，在某些公司，不管你多有能力，如果你年紀輕，就不會賦予你重大責任。但是聽說在這家公司，如果你能做，大家甚至連重要的工作都會交付給你。我想那是很有挑戰性的。還有，我有個朋友已經在這裡工作，所以我對這家公司有點了解。此外，我對汽車非常有興趣，而且我喜歡開發新的設計，所以我想我能替你們把工作做好。

I have heard that your company has a great benefits system and keeps regular office hours. And I'm sure that I can apply my professional skill in your company. So, I hope your company can give me a chance to realize my potential.

我已經聽說貴公司的福利制度很完善，而且上班時間固定。我確信我能在貴公司應用我的專業技術。所以，我希望貴公司能給我一個發揮潛力的機會。

面試者： What first got you interested in this type of occupation?

最先使你對這個行業產生興趣的是什麼？

應徵者： Well, I've always enjoyed writing. Even when I **was** little, I kept a diary, and I wrote in it every day. **And** I'm very curious and enjoy learning about things I **get** interested in. I like building up my own knowledge. And when I thought about how to use those sides **of** my personality, I decided to become a journalist.

嗯，我一直都很喜歡寫作，甚至從小就寫日記，而且每天寫。我對自己感興趣的事非常好奇，也很想知道。我喜歡增廣自己的見聞。而當我考慮到要如何應用我這方面的特質時，我決定要成為一名記者。

Well, I have to say that I love chi!dren. They are so cute and innocent. I like to teach them new things or play with them. I've wanted to be a kindergarten teacher since I was fifteen years old. I think this **job** can not only make me happy, but also make me **feel** fulfilled.

嗯，我必須說我很喜歡小孩。他們是如此的天真可愛。我喜歡教他們新東西，或陪他們玩。我從十五歲時，就想當幼稚園老師。我認為這份工作不但會使我快樂，還會令我感到充實。

面試者： What made you choose a company in this area, instead of one in Taipei?

是什麼原因使你選擇在這個地區的公司，而不是在台北？

應徵者： It was your location that attracted me the most. I was born and raised in Keelung, and now I want to find a job here, too, and settle down in this area.

最吸引我的是貴公司的地點。我在基隆出生，在基隆長大，所以現在我也想在這裡找份工作，並在這個地區定居下來。

I live in Taipei city for twenty-two years. After graduating from college, I think that I'm old enough to live by myself. So I decide to find a job in other city, and try to train myself by living without my family.

我在台北住了二十二年。大學畢業之後，我認為自己的年紀已經足以獨立生活了。所以我決定在其他城市找份工作，並試著在不和家人同住的情況下，訓練自己。

Major Subject · Graduation Thesis 主修·畢業論文

面試者： What was your major in college?
你大學主修什麼？

應徵者： Accounting. 會計。

I specialized in law. 我專攻法律。

I majored in economics. 我主修經濟。

I did mechanical engineering. 我唸機械工程。

I majored in electrical engineering. 我主修電機工程。

I majored in Chinese literature and minored in accounting. 我主修中文，輔修會計。

面試者： What was your graduation thesis on?
你畢業論文做什麼題目？

應徵者： I did my thesis on the differences between Chinese and American humor.
我的論文是關於中美幽默的差異。

I did some work on low-temperature superconductors.
我做了一些低溫超導體的研究。

I did a survey of changes in the educational system from the Han dynasty to the T'ang dynasty.
我研究漢代到唐代教育制度的變遷。

My graduation thesis was on the economical development of twenty-first century.
我的畢業論文是以二十一世紀的經濟發展為題。

面試者： What were your conclusions?
你有什麼結論？

應徵者： I found out several interesting things —— one was that my subject was too broad. I could have written a whole series of books and still not covered everything!
我發現幾件有趣的事 —— 其中之一是我的題目太大了，我可以寫上一整個系列的書，但卻仍無法包含每一樣東西！

I found out some really interesting things about the conductivity of liquid helium. I was sure I had a great discovery until my teacher told me the same discoveries had already been made fifteen years ago. (*laugh*) I think the most important thing I learned, though, was the importance of keeping good records.
我發現一些很有意思的事，那是關於液態氦的傳導性。我相信我有了重大的發現，直到後來我的老師告訴我說，同樣的發現在十五年前就有了。（笑）不過，我想我所學到的最重要的事就是，做好記錄是很重要的。

面試者： How do you think the education you've received will contribute to your work in this company?
你認為你所受的教育，對於你在本公司的工作有何助益？

應徵者： I think I have a good understanding of fundamentals in the areas your company deals with, and I can go on from here to build up the specific skills and knowledge I'll need to do my job well.
我想我對於貴公司的經營領域有充分的了解，我可以從這一點著手，開始增進做好工作必備的特殊技術與知識。

應徵者： I've already learned a lot in the classroom and I hope to be able to make practical use of it in business. Even if the job gets tough, I have a lot of confidence in my ability to see it through to the end.

我在課堂上已經學到很多東西，所以我希望能把它實際應用在商業上。即使這份工作很困難，我對於自己貫徹到底的能力還是很有信心。

Though I didn't major in accounting when I was a college student, I work part-time as an assistant to a professional accountant, and I have done this job for four years. Therefore, I'm very sure that I can perform well in your company.

雖然我大學時不是主修會計。但是我的兼職工作就是擔任一位專業會計師的助理，那份工作我已經做了四年了。因此，我十分肯定我在貴公司會表現得很好。

13 *Club and Group Activities* 社團與團體活動

面試者： Were you involved in any club activities at your university？ And if you were, what did you learn from them？

你大學時有沒有參加任何社團活動？如果有，你從中學到什麼？

應徵者： I was in a Bible study group. I'm a Christian, and that was a very good chance for me to learn more about Christ's teachings. And in my junior year, I was the leader of the group, which gave me a chance to try lots of things to build the circle up and bring in more people. It was a lot of work, but I learned a lot about working with people and I think that will be useful after I graduate.

我參加聖經研習團。我是基督徒，而那對我來說是個很好的機會，讓我可以學到更多的基督教義。我大三時擔任團長，所以我有機會嘗試許多方法來鞏固團契，和引進更多人。事情很多，但是我也學到和別人一起工作的方法，我想那在我畢業之後會成為有用的經驗。

I was in the judo club, and got Second Dan rank during my sophomore year. Judo practice is very good for teaching spiritual and mental harmony, I think.

我參加柔道社，並在大二時得到二段。我想，柔道練習對訓練精神與心理的和諧非常有用。

應徵者： I was in the tennis club for four years. That was a good experience and I got a lot out of it. In particular, it gave me confidence in my ability to see things through, even if they aren't easy. That will be useful all my life, I think.

我在網球社待了四年，那是個很好的經驗，而且我在那裡學到很多。尤其是它使我對自己的能力有信心，相信自己能看清事情，即使那並不容易。我想那對我而言是終生受用的。

I was in a singing club. We put on quite a few concerts, and I learned a great deal about the importance of teamwork. That was a good experience.

我參加合唱團。我們舉辦了好幾場音樂會，所以我學到很多關於團隊合作的重要性。那是個很好的經驗。

I didn't join a club, but some friends and I formed a group we called "Friends of Cycling", and every Sunday we got together for a bicycle ride somewhere.

我沒有參加社團，但是我和幾個朋友組了一個團，我們叫它「單車之友」，每個星期天，我們都會聚在某個地方騎腳踏車。

14 ▶ *Part-time Jobs* 工 讀

面試者：Did you work during college? 你大學時有工作嗎？

應徵者：Yes, I delivered newspapers all through summer vacation during my sophomore year.
有，我大二時，整個暑假都在送報紙。

Yes, every year during winter vacation I worked as a department store delivery boy.
有，我每年寒假都在百貨公司做送貨員。

I did some English tutoring with high school students for two years. 我當了兩年的英文家教，是教高中生。

No, I always traveled during summer and winter vacation when I was in college.
沒有，當我還在唸大學時，我寒暑假都會去旅行。

面試者：What did you do with the money you earned?
你怎麼用你賺的錢?

應徵者：I used it to help with living expenses.
我用它來補貼生活費。

I'd been wanting some scuba-diving equipment for a long time. I used the money for that.
我想要一些水肺潛水裝備已經很久了，於是就用這筆錢來買。

I like to travel, so I saved up the money for that.
我喜歡旅行，所以就把錢存起來旅行。

⑮ Qualifications 資 格

面試者： What do you think about your qualifications for this position? 你認為就這份工作而言，你的資格如何？

應徵者： I know a lot about how the Taiwanese economy works, and how business is done here. And I'm a hard worker when I have something challenging to do. 我對台灣的經濟運作方式，以及交易方式懂得很多。而且遇到有挑戰性的工作時，我會非常努力。

Although I have no work experience, I think that I'm a reliable person. And I promise that I'll do my best in this position. 我雖然沒有工作經驗，但我認為自己是個可以信賴的人。而且我保證，我會盡全力來做這份工作。

面試者： Can you make yourself understood in English without too much difficulty? 你可以用英文表達清楚，而沒有太大的困難嗎？

應徵者： Yes, I think I am quite fluent in English. 是的，我想我的英文相當流利。

面試者： Can you use a computer? 你會用電腦嗎？

應徵者： Yes, I can use Word, Excel, and PowerPoint. 會，我會用 Word、Excel 和 PowerPoint。

面試者： What are your qualifications for being a flight attendant? 你有什麼資格，可以擔任空服員這份工作？

應徵者： People say that I'm a considerate and adaptable person. And I think with your company's training, I can be a professional flight attendant. Furthermore, I like to travel anywhere in the world, so I consider myself a suitable person for this job.

大家都說我是個體貼而且適應力強的人。我認為經過貴公司的訓練之後，我就能成為專業的空服員。此外，我喜歡到世界各地旅遊，所以我認為自己適合從事這份工作。

面試者： Do you have any special skills?
你有任何特殊技能嗎？

應徵者： I graduated from Tainan National College of the Arts, so I'm proficient in painting and using art software like Photoshop, Illustrator and CorelDraw.

我畢業於國立台南藝術學院，所以我精通繪畫和美術軟體的應用，像是 Photoshop、Illustrator 和 CorelDraw。

My father is an architect, and so I naturally got interested in architecture when I was quite young. Recently I've done some blueprints and designing for my father, and have been helping him, so I know something about architecture.

我爸爸是個建築師，所以我從很小的時候，就自然而然地對建築感興趣。最近我替我父親完成了一些藍圖和設計，而且一直都在幫他的忙，所以我懂一些建築方面的東西。

面試者： Do you have any licenses or other special
qualifications?
你有任何執照，或其他特殊資格嗎？

應徵者： I have a driver's license and an architecture license.
我有駕照和建築師執照。

I've passed the tests of risk management.
我已經通過風險管理師的考試。

I got 850 points in TOEIC test, and I have teacher's
qualifications.
我在多益測驗中拿到 850 分，而且我擁有教師資格。

面試者： I see by your resume that you have been doing office
work? 我從你的履歷表上得知，你一直都有在上班？

應徵者： Yes, I have worked at the Crown Oil Company for
three years. 是的，我在皇冠石油公司做了三年。

Yes, I have worked at the Daedo Trading Company
for two years.
是的，我在狄多貿易公司工作了兩年。

16 Questions About the Company ・ 有關公司的問題

面試者： Tell me what you know about our company.

告訴我你對我們公司知道多少。

應徵者： Well, the company was founded in Chicago in 1946 by Henry Ward, who was the first president. It's capitalized at 50 billion, employs 8,500 people, and is the largest-or maybe the second largest-company in its field in the States. The president is now James Weed. He is the second president, after Mr. Ward. Since last year, the company has been putting a lot of effort into exporting petroleum products.

嗯，貴公司是在 1946 年時，由亨利・華德先生在芝加哥所創立的，他是首任總裁。公司的資金有 500 億，員工有 8,500 人，而且在美國，是這個行業中第一大或第二大的公司。現任總裁是詹姆士・韋德先生。他是繼華德先生之後的第二任總裁。從去年開始，貴公司一直致力於外銷石油產品。

面試者： Do you know what companies are stockholders in this company?

你知道這家公司的股東是哪些公司嗎？

應徵者： Yes, the main stockholders are FF Chemical Industry and Continental Motors.

知道，主要的股東是 FF 化學工業和大陸汽車公司。

面試者： Do you know anything about our related enterprises?
你對於本公司的關係企業有任何了解嗎？

應徵者： Yes, in addition to the main business — food production, your company also has one hundred and eighty convenience stores. Besides, you have also invested in cyber cafes.
是的，除了主要的業務 —— 食品業之外，貴公司還有 180 家便利商店。此外，你們還有投資網咖。

面試者： What do you know about our major products and our share of the market?
你對我們的主要產品和市場佔有率了解多少？

應徵者： Your company's products are mostly marketed in Europe and the United States, but have sold particularly well here in Taiwan, so I think in the future you'll find Taiwan to be a profitable market, too. It's said that you are one of the major producers in your field.
貴公司的產品大多外銷歐美，但在台灣這裡的銷路卻特別好，所以我想你們將來會發現，台灣也是個有利可圖的市場。據說貴公司是這個行業的主要製造商之一。

Your major products are digital cameras and cell phones. And your company has two thirds of the Asian cell phone market. In Taiwan, you are the biggest technology company.
貴公司的主要產品是數位相機和手機。而且貴公司還佔有三分之二的亞洲手機市場。在台灣，貴公司是規模最大的科技公司。

⑰ *General Knowledge* 常 識

面試者： Do you know what UN is an abbreviation for?
你知道 UN 這個縮寫代表什麼嗎？

應徵者： It stands for (the) United Nations.
它代表 United Nations（聯合國）。

面試者： Which countries are members of the European Union?
哪些國家是歐盟的成員？

應徵者： France, Germany, Italy, Belgium, the Netherlands,
Luxemburg, Great Britain, Ireland, Denmark, Greece,
Finland, Portugal, Sweden, Spain. Fourteen
countries altogether.
法國、德國、義大利、比利時、荷蘭、盧森堡、英國、愛
爾蘭、丹麥、希臘、芬蘭、葡萄牙、瑞典、西班牙。總共
十四個國家。

面試者： Do you know what the WTO is and what its main
goal is?
你知道 WTO 是什麼嗎？其主要目標為何？

應徵者： WTO means World Trade Organization, and its main
goal is to regulate international trade.
WTO 的意思是世界貿易組織，它的主要目標是管理國際貿
易。

面試者： Why does Taiwan want to be part of the WTO?

台灣為什麼要加入 WTO？

應徵者： Because if Taiwan is a member of the WTO, we can enjoy the Most Favored Nation Status of other countries. And that'll be a big help to our export trade. But we have to open our market to other members, too.

因為如果台灣成為 WTO 的會員，我們就可以享有其他國家的最惠國待遇。而那會對我們的出口貿易大有幫助。但我們同樣也必須將市場開放給其他會員國。

面試者： What are the two basic causes of inflation?

通貨膨脹的兩個基本原因是什麼？

應徵者： Well, when the demand exceeds the supply, people will spend more money to buy a product, which makes the price rise. That is so-called demand-pull inflation. On the other hand, when the cost of the product goes up, which makes the supply decrease, then the price will rise again. And that means there is cost-push inflation. These are the two basic causes of inflation.

嗯，當需求超過供給時，人們會花更多的錢來買一項產品，因此使得價格上漲。那就是所謂的需求拉動的通貨膨脹。另一方面，當產品的成本提高時，會使得供給減少，然後價格將會再度上漲。而那就表示有成本推動的通貨膨脹。這就是通貨膨脹的兩個基本原因。

⟨18⟩ *Current Topics* 時下話題

面試者： There's been a lot in the newspapers recently on "stagflation". Do you know what that means?

最近報紙上常提到「停滯型通貨膨脹」，你知道那是什麼意思嗎？

應徵者： That describes a situation where the economy is stagnant and there is inflation at the same time. Journalists combined "stagnation" and "inflation" and came up with "stagflation".

那是描述一個經濟蕭條與通貨膨脹同時發生的情況。記者把「停滯」和「通貨膨脹」結合起來，成為「停滯型通貨膨脹」。

面試者： The stock market puts out the Dow Jones Average every day. Do you know what that is?

股票市場每天都算出道瓊工業平均指數，你知道那是什麼嗎？

應徵者： Yes, the Dow is the average price of stocks for that day, computed according to the methods of the Dow Jones Company in the United States.

知道，那是當天的股票平均價格，依照美國道瓊斯公司的方法來計算。

面試者： Do you know what EPS means?

你知道 EPS 代表什麼嗎？

應徵者： It means Earnings Per Share. It amounts to the net profit after tax divided by the number of shares of common stocks.

它的意思是每股盈餘。也就等於稅後淨利除以普通股股數。

面試者： The problem between China and Taiwan is getting more and more attention. Can you explain the difference between their political conceptions?

中國大陸和台灣之間的問題，已經引起愈來愈多的注意。你可以解釋它們的政治理念有何不同嗎？

應徵者： OK, I think the most important difference is that China insists there is only one China. And they talk about everything according to this rule. But Taiwan wants one country on each side of the strait. So they still can't agree politically now.

好的，我認為最重要的差別是在於，中國大陸堅持只有一個中國。而且根據這個原則的話，任何問題都可以談。但台灣卻想要海峽兩岸一邊一國。所以它們至今仍無法取得政治上的共識。

⟨19⟩ *Views on Work* 對工作的看法

面試者： Tell me what you think a job is.

告訴我你認為工作是什麼。

應徵者： Well, a way to make a living, of course, but beyond that I think a job is a way of developing as a person.

嗯，工作當然是一種謀生的方式，但除此之外，我想工作是一個人成長的途徑。

I think when a man finds a job he really wants to do, he's found a treasure to last him all his life. Of course, it's also a heavy responsibility, and not always easy.

我想，當一個人找到他真正想做的工作時，他就找到了可以支撐他一輩子的寶藏。當然，那也是個重責大任，而且未必是容易的。

A lot of people say that a job for a woman is just a place where she sits for a while. But even if I don't continue working all my life, while I am working I want to do the best job I can and learn as much as I can.

很多人說，工作對女人來說，只是一個暫時停留的地方。但是即使我不會工作一輩子，在我工作時，我還是會盡力把它做好，並盡我所能地學習。

I think a job is a big responsibility.　Once you take on a job, then you should try your best to finish it. And to me, seeking achievement and enjoying my job are equally important.

我認為工作是一個很重大的責任。一旦你接下了一份工作，那麼你就必須盡力去完成它。而且對我來說，尋求成就感和樂於工作是同等重要的。

⑳ *Personal Outlook* 個人的看法

面試者： Between work and family, which is more important to you?

工作和家庭，何者對你而言比較重要？

應徵者： Family is more important, but with a happy family, you can do your job better.

家庭比較重要，但擁有幸福的家庭，會使你的工作表現更加出色。

面試者： What do you think is the most important thing for your happiness?

你認為對你的幸福而言，最重要的是什麼？

應徵者： I think the most important thing is having good friends. A person can't live by himself, I think. It takes a lot of people working and cooperating together. It's really important to have good friends you can talk to, and the more really good friends I have, the better.

我認為最重要的是有要好的朋友。我想一個人無法獨自生活。需要有很多人一起工作和合作。有可以談話的好朋友真的很重要，而且我認為，真正的好朋友越多越好。

面試者： What kind of things do you want from your job?

你想從工作中得到什麼？

應徵者： I've wanted to be involved in engineering ever since I was little. If I pass this interview (*smile*) and am accepted by this company, I want to contribute whatever I can to improving technology and building better ships. I want to be professional in my field.

我從小就想從事工程方面的工作。如果我通過這次的面試（微笑），且被貴公司錄用的話，我會盡我所能來改良技術，以造出更好的船。我想成為這個領域的專家。

面試者： What do you think about overtime work?

你對於加班的看法如何？

應徵者： I think it's inevitable. As long as there is reasonable compensation, I'll be willing to work overtime.

我認為那是無法避免的。只要有合理的補償，我會很樂意加班的。

21 *Why You Changed Your Job* · 為什麼換工作

面試者： What made you decide to change jobs?

是什麼原因使你決定換工作？

應徵者： I would like to get a job in which I can have good opportunity for advancement.

我想找一個有良好升遷機會的工作。

I find the job here very challenging.

我覺得這裡的工作很有挑戰性。

I hope to get a job that will let me use what I've learned in college.

我希望能找到一份工作，讓我可以運用在大學所學到的東西。

面試者： Didn't you like the work?

你不喜歡那份工作嗎？

應徵者： Yes, some of it I enjoyed very much. But economically it's fairly unstable.

不是的，有些地方我很喜歡，但是就經濟上來說，那份工作相當不穩定。

應徵者：No, I think I'm a very outgoing and energetic person. But my last job was really dull work. I believe I should find a job as a salesman.

是的，我認為自己是個非常外向而充滿活力的人。但我上一份工作真的非常單調乏味。我相信我應該找一份業務員的工作。

面試者：May I ask you why you left the company?

我可以問你為什麼離開那家公司嗎？

應徵者：I didn't think there was any opportunity for advancement there.

我認為那裡沒有什麼升遷的機會。

My health was quite frail some years ago and I couldn't bear the work pressure at that time.

幾年前我的身體相當虛弱，而且我當時無法承受工作壓力。

22 *Applications to Other Companies* 申請其他公司

面試者： Have you applied for work with any other companies?
你有去別家公司應徵嗎？

應徵者： No, this is the only one. 沒有，這是唯一的一家。

Yes, I also applied at AS Co., in case I wasn't accepted here. The company is smaller, but the work is very similar.
有，我還應徵了 AS 公司，以免貴公司沒有錄取我。那家公司比較小，但是工作內容很類似。

Yes, I applied to AS Co., but that was just to get experience in being interviewed. It would be hard to develop my abilities in such a large company, I think. That's why I want to work for this company.
是的，我還應徵了 AS 公司，但那只是為了要得到面試的經驗。我想，在那麼大的公司工作，不容易培養自己的能力，所以我想替貴公司工作。

面試者： What were the results? 結果怎樣？

應徵者： I took the sales executive examination, but I haven't heard the results yet.
我參加了行銷主管考試，但是還不知道結果。

I was offered a position at AS Co.
AS 公司給了我一份工作。

(*smile*) They turned me down. （微笑）我沒被錄取。

面試者： Why do you think you didn't get the job?

你想你為什麼沒有得到那份工作？

應徵者： I was nervous, and I couldn't express myself the way I wanted to.

我很緊張，所以無法照我想要的方式來表達我自己。

I'm not very sure, but I guess the reason is that I don't have enough practical experience.

我不是很確定，但我猜想，沒被錄取是因為我的實際經驗不足。

面試者： If you are accepted at both places, which company will you choose?

如果你兩邊都被錄取，你會選哪家公司？

應徵者： This one, of course. Your company is my first choice. I want to work for you.

當然是這家。貴公司是我的優先選擇，我想為你們工作。

23 Aspirations After Entering the Company 進公司後的期望

面試者： If you join this company, what section would you
like to work in?
如果你進入本公司，你會想到哪個部門工作？

應徵者： If possible, I'd like you to try me in the international
section. 如果可能的話，我希望您讓我到國際部門試試看。
= I'd like to work in the international section.
我想在國際部門工作。

In the general affairs section. 在一般事務部門。

In the accounting section. 在會計部門。

In the business section. 在營業部門。

In the planning department. 在企畫部。

In the publicity department. 在宣傳部。

In the promotion department. 在公關宣傳部。

面試者： What starting salary would you expect?
你希望起薪多少？

應徵者： I'd like to start at about NT27,000 a month.
我希望起薪是一個月兩萬七千元左右。

I have to take care of my family, so I'd like to start
at around NT30,000 a month.
我得照顧我的家庭，所以我想從月薪三萬左右開始。

It depends on your company's salary system.
依照貴公司的薪水制度。

面試者： How long does it take to get here from your home?
從你家到這裡要多久？

應徵者： It takes about 40 minutes. 大約需要四十分鐘。
It takes about an hour and ten minutes.
大約需要一小時又十分鐘。

If I get this job, I'll move to a new apartment nearby.
如果我得到這份工作，我將搬到這附近的一棟新公寓。

面試者： That's quite a way. Are you planning to find a
boarding house nearby, or do you have relatives you
can stay with?
路途很遠。你有打算在附近找個寄宿的地方，還是有親
戚可以一起住？

應徵者： I think I can commute that far without any trouble.
I'm pretty strong.
我想我能通勤，這個距離對我而言不是問題，我相當強壯。

Yes, I have relatives living about thirty minutes from
here, so I'm planning to stay with them for a while.
是的，我有親戚住在離這裡約三十分鐘的地方，所以我打
算和他們一起住一陣子。

面試者： How do you get here? 你是怎麼到這裡來的？

應徵者： I take the bus. 我搭公車。
I take the train. 我坐火車。
I walk. 我走路。
I drive my car. 我開車過來的。

面試者： Are there any particular conditions that you would
like the company to take into consideration?
你有任何需要公司列入考慮的特殊情況嗎？

應徵者： No, nothing in particular.
沒有，沒有什麼特殊情況。

㉔ How Long You Can Work ‧ 可以做多久

面試者： How long do you think that we can depend on your working here?

你想你會在本公司待多久？

應徵者： If I like the job and I feel I am making progress in the work, I would stay until I reach the age limit.

如果我喜歡這份工作，而且覺得自己在工作中有所進步的話，我會一直待到退休年齡。

面試者： You are single now, but what will you do when you get married?

你目前是單身，但是你結婚之後打算怎麼辦？

應徵者： I've thought about that lot. I know a lot of women take a job, planning to make a career of it, and then they change their mind. But I'm hoping to make it my lifetime work. So if I get married, I will find some way that I can continue my work, too.

關於這件事我已經考慮了很多。我知道有很多女人有工作，而且打算在工作上好好發展，但是後來又改變主意。可是我卻希望把這份工作當成終生的職業。所以如果我結婚，我也會找到可以繼續工作的方式。

應徵者： First, I'm not going to get married before twenty-eight years old. And that is six years from now. Second, I'm sure that I won't quit the job. Your company's welfare system is excellent, and there's no better choice.

首先，我並不會在二十八歲以前結婚，而那距離現在還有六年的時間。其次，我確定自己不會主動辭掉這份工作。貴公司的福利制度很棒，已經沒有更好的選擇了。

25 *How to Contact You* 聯絡方式

面試者： How can we get in touch with you? 我們怎麼聯絡你？

應徵者： I can be reached at home in the evening. My telephone number is 2707-5545.

我晚上會在家裡，我的電話號碼是 2707-5545。

You can send an e-mail. My e-mail address is wanglien@hinet.com.tw

你可以寄電子郵件給我。我的電子郵件地址為 wangiien @hinet.com.tw。

面試者： How can I contact you about our decision?

我怎麼把我們的決定通知你？

應徵者： You can call me at this number between four and six in the afternoon: (02) 2707-5545.

你可以在下午四點到六點打這個號碼：(02) 2707-5545。

面試者： May I call you at home about our final decision?

我可以打電話到你家，通知你我們最後的決定嗎？

應徵者： Yes, please. My phone number is 2932-4567.

可以，請打電話通知我。我的電話號碼是 2932-4567。

面試者： Shall we notify you of our decision by mail or phone?

我們要寄信還是打電話通知你我們的決定？

應徵者： By telephone, please. 請打電話。

By mail, please. 請寄信。

26 ▸ *Any Questions?* 有什麼問題？

面試者： Do you have any questions you would like to ask me?
你有任何問題想問嗎？

應徵者： What hours would I work？ 上班時間是什麼時候？

May I ask about the pay? 我可以請教薪水是多少嗎？

Would I have to work overtime very often?
我得常常加班嗎？

Would there be any opportunities to work abroad in
the future? 將來有機會到國外工作嗎？

May I ask how much the bonuses are?
我可以問紅利有多少嗎？

面試者： You may ask questions about us if you have any.
你如果對我們有任何問題，都可以問。

應徵者： Sure. What would my job entail?
好。我需要做什麼工作？

May I ask if there is any pre-service training or in-
service training in your company?
我可以請教，貴公司有任何職前訓練或在職訓練嗎？

How long is the trial period?
試用期是多久？

第②篇 ▶ 求職實況會話

English Conversation for Job Interview

1. Secretary in a Foreign Capital Company

The Overseas Investment Consultant Company is looking for a secretary for the office manager. They called National Taipei College of Business and asked them to recommend one of their recent graduates. The school sent Miss Wang's personal history to them and arranged for an interview. Now Miss Wang is being interviewed by Mr. Davis, the office manager.

(*D* : *Mr. Davis*　*W* : *Miss Wang*)

D : What was your best subject in college?

W : Financial Management. I majored in finance, and I think Financial Management was the most interesting subject.

D : What kind of job are you interested in?

W : I want a job which is related to what I've learned in college. And I would also like to be able to have some responsibility in my work.

D : I can appreciate that. I would expect my secretary to be able to work independently and take over some of my ordinary responsibilities such as answering routine correspondence, taking phone calls for me, and sometimes assisting me with business affairs.

W : Yes, I see. In my previous job, I did typing and filing and answered phone calls every day.

1. 外商公司秘書

「海外投資顧問公司」正在替公司的經理找一位秘書，它們打電話給「國立台北商業技術學院」，請它們推薦一個最近畢業的學生。學校把王小姐的履歷表寄給它們，並安排了一次面談。現在王小姐正在和公司經理戴維斯先生面談。

（D：戴維斯先生　W：王小姐）

戴維斯：妳大學時最優秀的科目是哪一科？

王小姐：財務管理。我主修金融，而我認為財務管理是最有趣的科目。

戴維斯：妳對哪一種工作有興趣？

王小姐：我想要找一個和所學相關的工作，也希望能在工作上負起一些責任。

戴維斯：我了解妳的想法，我會希望我的秘書能夠獨立作業，並接管我的一些平常事務，像是回覆日常書信，替我接電話，還有有時候要幫我處理業務。

王小姐：是的，我知道。在我的前一份工作中，我每天都要打字、把文件歸檔和接電話。

D : Do you have any accounting or secretarial experience?

W : Yes. Two years ago, I had a part-time job as an administrative assistant. I did that job for one year.

D : Are you adept in English listening and speaking?

W : Mm, I think I can handle ordinary conversation without any problems.

D : Good. Have you had any experience as a guide?

W : Well, not exactly. But I have shown some of my foreign friends around Taipei.

D : Once in a while we have visitors from abroad and I would like to be able to ask my secretary to take them shopping and sightseeing.

W : I think I would like that.

D : I see. We work a five-day week and there is rarely any overtime. The salary would be NT26,000 to start and raises would be given according to your ability.

D : In your opinion, how's your ability to handle stress?

W : Well, when I was in college, I had to handle both schoolwork and my part-time job. I always needed to make good use of the 24 hours in a day. Sometimes I felt really stressed, but I could generally overcome that kind of feeling.

戴維斯：妳有任何會計或秘書的經驗嗎？

王小姐：有的，我兩年前打工時，當過行政助理。我那份工作做了一年。

戴維斯：妳精通英語的聽和說嗎？

王小姐：嗯，我想要應付平常的對話是沒有問題的。

戴維斯：很好。妳有任何當導遊的經驗嗎？

王小姐：嗯，不算真的有，但是我曾經帶我的一些外國朋友在台北四處遊覽。

戴維斯：我們偶爾會有從國外來的訪客，我希望能請我的秘書帶他們去購物和觀光。

王小姐：我想我會喜歡做那些事。

戴維斯：我明白了。我們每週工作五天，很少加班，起薪兩萬六，會根據妳的能力來加薪。

戴維斯：依妳之見，妳的抗壓能力如何？

王小姐：嗯，當我還在唸技術學院時，我必須同時應付學校課業和打工。我總是得善用一天中的 24 小時。有時候真的會覺得壓力很大，但一般來說，我都能克服那種感覺。

D : Well, how do you feel about the job, Miss Wang?

W : I think it sounds like what I am looking for.

D : Thank you. You should be hearing from us within a few days.

W : Thank you, Mr. Davis.

Executive secretary

The Administrative Division of the State Controller's Office has a Female executive secretarial position available. Minimum requirements are:

· Chinese Typing-70 wpm
· Computer-word, Excel, PowerPoint
· Age-20~28

Interested applicants should mail applications and resumes to:

    Controller of Public Accts.
    Personnel Office
    111 E. 19th Street
    Salt Lake City, Utah

戴維斯： 嗯，王小姐，妳覺得這份工作如何？

王小姐： 我想這聽起來就像是我正在找的工作。

戴維斯： 謝謝。幾天之內妳就會收到我們的消息。

王小姐： 謝謝你，戴維斯先生。

2. *Trading Company*

The Central Trading Company put an ad in the newspaper as follows:

We need English-speaking men with 2 or more years of sales experience under the age of 35. Marketing knowledge helpful. Send resume (English and Chinese).

Mr. Yang, who has been working for Dah Hsin Trading Company, applied for that job. An interview was arranged between Mr. Yang and Mr. Miles, the sales manager.

(*M* : *Mr. Miles* *Y* : *Mr. Yang*)

M : Please make yourself at home. Smoke if you like.

Y : Thank you.

M : To start with, may I ask why you are interested in working at our company?

Y : First, you have had an impressive growth record, ever since Mr. Peter Mitchell founded the company 35 years ago. Second, marketing is obviously very important for you and I will have a great deal to learn from and contribute to your company.

M : Very well. You are now with Dah Hsin Company. What is your chief responsibility there?

Y : I am in charge of organizing trade conferences for distributors held in different parts of the nation almost every month.

2. 貿易公司

「中央貿易公司」在報上登了以下這則廣告：

　　我們需要會說英語的男性，須有兩年以上的銷售經驗，年三十五以下。具行銷知識者尤佳。請寄中英履歷表來應徵。

楊先生一直在「大新貿易公司」工作，他去應徵了那份工作。他和業務經理邁爾斯先生安排了一場面談。

（*M*：邁爾斯先生　*Y*：楊先生）

邁爾斯：　請不要客氣，想抽煙的話也可以。

楊先生：　謝謝。

邁爾斯：　首先，想請問你為什麼會對在本公司工作有興趣？

楊先生：　第一，從彼得‧米歇爾先生在三十五年前創立貴公司之後，貴公司一直都有很出色的業績成長。第二，市場行銷對貴公司而言，顯然非常重要，所以我在這裡將會學到很多東西，並對貴公司有所貢獻。

邁爾斯：　很好，你目前是在「大新公司」工作，你在那邊的主要職務是什麼？

楊先生：　我負責在全國不同的地區，替經銷商安排貿易會議，幾乎每個月都有。

M : Are you well acquainted with English? Most of our customers are from the U.S.A. and England, so we need a professional staff to communicate or negotiate with them.

Y : Trust me, I can cope with that. I got 780 points in TOEIC test. And I'm a diplomatic person, so I'm sure that I can manage it.

M : Have you ever managed export business?

Y : No, never. But I'm willing to learn everything. Moreover, I'm really interested in international trade.

M : You may ask question about us, if you have any.

Y : Sure. What would my job entail?

M : This fall, we will launch a new product. At the beginning, you need to report to me about all marketing activities. Then there will be a lot of work and you may be called in on weekends. I'll tell you the details if you are qualified for this job. What salary would you expect to get?

Y : I expect a salary in accordance with your company's regulations. By the way, how often do you adjust an employee's salary?

M : It depends on his performance. But in general, we will appraise each employee's ability twice a year.

Y : Well, I don't have any more questions.

M : OK, you will be hearing from us within ten days.

Y : Thank you.

邁爾斯： 你精通英文嗎？我們公司大部分的客戶是來自美國和英國，所以我們需要一位專業的職員，好跟他們溝通或交涉。

楊先生： 相信我，我可以應付那些事。我在多益測驗中拿到了780分。而且我是個善於交際的人，我確定我可以做好這些事。

邁爾斯： 你曾接辦出口事務嗎？

楊先生： 不，從來沒有。但我很願意學習每一件事。還有，我對國際貿易很有興趣。

邁爾斯： 你對本公司有任何問題的話，可以提出來問。

楊先生： 好。我需要做哪些工作？

邁爾斯： 我們將在今年秋天推出新產品。一開始，你需要向我報告和行銷活動有關的所有事務。之後會有很多工作要做，而且你可能會在週末時被叫來上班。如果你有被錄取的話，我會再告訴你詳細的情況。你的理想待遇是多少？

楊先生： 依公司規定。順便問一下，公司多久會調一次員工的薪水？

邁爾斯： 看個人表現。但一般來說，我們每年會考核員工的能力兩次。

楊先生： 嗯，我沒有其他問題了。

邁爾斯： 好，你會在十天之內接到我們的消息。

楊先生： 謝謝。

3. Foreign Bank Staff Member

Citibank in Taipei called the Vocational Bureau of Taiwan University because they were seeking a trainee. The employment bureau sent Lee Chung-hsin to talk with the bank manager, Mr. Warren.

(*W* : *Mr. Warren* *L* : *Lee Chung-hsin*)

W : I see by your resume that you have just graduated from college. I assume you haven't had any working experience. Is that right?

L : That's right. I've only had some part-time jobs working in department stores.

W : Well, experience is not important in this job. We are looking for a man we can train to be a financial planner. By the way, are you interested in investment?

L : Yes, I bought several stocks when I was in college. And I did make some money by this kind of investment.

W : We are more interested in finding someone who is alert and quick at figures. Do you like meeting the public?

L : Yes, I enjoy working with people.

3. 外銀職員

「花旗銀行台北分行」打電話給「台大就業輔導處」，因為它們要找一位儲備幹部。就業輔導處讓李忠信前往和銀行經理華倫先生會談。

（*W*：華倫先生　*L*：李忠信）

華　倫：我從你的履歷表上知道，你剛從大學畢業，我想你沒有任何工作經驗，對不對？

李忠信：對，我只在百貨公司打過工。

華　倫：嗯，經驗對這個工作而言並不重要，我們要找的是可以訓練成理財專員的人。順便一提，你對投資有興趣嗎？

李忠信：有，我大學時買過幾張股票，而且也真的靠這種投資賺了一些錢。

華　倫：我們比較想要找個對數字靈敏，且反應又快的人。你喜歡跟大眾接觸嗎？

李忠信：喜歡，我喜歡和人們一起工作。

W : We have very pleasant working conditions and I think we have a fine staff to work with. You would be assigned an experienced employee to help you. He would be responsible for training you.

L : About how long would it take to become a qualified financial planner?

W : It depends on one's effort and practical experience. Some become good financial planners within three months. It takes as long as two or three years for some to become good at it. Moreover, ability in speaking and understanding English is very important. Have you studied English conversation?

L : Yes, I had an American tutor for two years. I had a lesson with her twice a week. Would I be using English every day in this job?

W : Yes, many of our customers are Americans, so you would be speaking English with most of them. Do you know anything about various kinds of insurance funds?

L : No, I'm afraid I don't. I'd be glad to learn.

W : That's a good answer. I appreciate your being frank.

L : I'm glad to hear that.

W : Well, we will keep in touch with you. I appreciate your interest in the job.

L : It has been a pleasure talking with you, Mr. Warren. Thank you.

華　倫：本公司有非常舒適的工作環境，而且我認為我們也有很
　　　　優秀的同事一起工作。我們會派一個有經驗的人來幫
　　　　你，而且他會負責訓練你。

李忠信：大概要多久才能成為一位合格的理財專員？

華　倫：那要看個人的努力和實務經驗，有的人在三個月之內就
　　　　成為很優秀理財專員；有些人則要兩三年才會熟練。
　　　　外此，英文的口說及理解能力也非常重要。你學過英語
　　　　會話嗎？

李忠信：學過，我和一位美國家庭教師學了兩年，每個禮拜上兩
　　　　次課。做這份工作需要每天講英文嗎？

華　倫：是的，我們很多顧客都是美國人，所以你要和絕大多數
　　　　的顧客說英文。你對於各種保險基金有任何了解嗎？

李忠信：不，我恐怕不懂，我會很樂意學習。

華　倫：答得好，我欣賞你的坦白。

李忠信：我也很高興聽你這麼說。

華　倫：嗯，我們會和你保持聯絡，我欣賞你對這份工作的興趣。

李忠信：和你談話很愉快，華倫先生，謝謝你。

4. Editor on an English Magazine

Ivy League Analytical English magazine advertised for an English editor. They asked the applicants to send their personal histories in essay form. Mr. Wu has been granted an interview with Mr. Bacon, who is the managing editor.

(*B* : *Mr. Bacon* *W* : *Mr. Wu*)

B : Please sit down.

W : Thank you.

B : After reading over your resume, I guess your English is quite good. Have you had any experience in the writing field?

W : No, I haven't had any professional experience, but I have always been interested in creative writing.

B : I know your major subject was English Literature, but I wonder what your favorite subject is.

W : Well, besides English, I also enjoyed Chinese literature and my poetry class. I appreciate the originality of English poems and the sentiment of Chinese poems.

4. 英文雜誌編輯

「長春藤英語解析雜誌」登報徵求英文編輯，他們要求應徵者要以文章的形式寄履歷表來。吳先生獲准和總編輯培根先生會談。

（**B**：培根先生　**W**：吳先生）

培　　根：請坐。

吳先生：謝謝。

培　　根：看過你的履歷表之後，我猜想你的英文一定相當不錯。你在寫作方面有沒有任何經驗？

吳先生：沒有，我沒有任何專業經驗，但是我一向對於創作很有興趣。

培　　根：我知道你的主修科目是英國文學，但我想知道你最喜歡的科目是什麼？

吳先生：嗯，除了英文，我還喜歡上中國文學和詩作的課。我很欣賞英詩的創意與中國詩的多愁善感。

B : Why are you applying for this job?

W : Mm, my college teacher was an American. She was also our adviser on our English language newspaper. I was the editor for two years. During that time, I took to editing just like a duck to water. I really enjoyed that job, so I wish to be an English editor in the future.

B : That's very interesting. Please tell me what you did exactly.

W : Well, I planned the layout of the newspaper and then I assigned various articles and columns to my schoolmates to write. I wrote the front-page story each time.

B : What is your aim in going into the field of publishing?

W : To be frank with you, I would like nothing better than to be a chief editor some day.

B : That can be a rough job, you know.

W : Yes, I know that. But I like adventure and excitement as well as writing.

培　根：你為什麼想應徵這份工作？

吳先生：嗯，我的大學老師是美國人，她也是我們英文報紙的
　　　　顧問，我做了兩年的編輯。在那段時間裡，我編輯時
　　　　就像是如魚得水般，我真的很喜歡那份工作，所以我
　　　　希望將來可以成為英文編輯。

培　根：很有意思。請把你做的事全都告訴我。

吳先生：嗯，我設計報紙的版面，然後分配各種文章和專欄給
　　　　其他同學寫，我每次都寫頭版新聞。

培　根：你進入出版業有什麼目標？

吳先生：坦白說，我只想有一天能成為主編。

培　根：你應該知道那是個很辛苦的工作吧。

吳先生：是的，我知道，但是我喜歡冒險、刺激和寫作。

B : Well, working in an editorial office may not be exciting enough for you. What do you think?

W : I would be glad to do routine work, if I could be assured of making advancements in the future.

B : I think this type of position would be a very good start for you. I am quite sure we can work something out for you, but I cannot give you a definite answer today. We will let you know within just a few days.

W : Fine. Thank you very much, Mr. Bacon.

JOURNALIST/EDITORIAL ASST. Leading New Year newspaper seeks trainee for Int'l News Division. B.A.(preferable in journalism) required; college newspaper experience desirable. Possibility of travel Excellent benefits. Send resume to Publisher, P.O. Box 720, New York, New York 10073.

培　根：那麼，在編輯室工作對你來說可能不夠刺激。你覺
　　　　得呢？

吳先生：如果能確保將來有所發展，那麼我也喜歡做例行的
　　　　工作。

培　根：我想這種職位對你而言，會是個很好的開始，我確
　　　　信我們可以替你想辦法，但是我今天無法給你一個
　　　　明確的答覆。我們幾天之內就會讓你知道。

吳先生：好，非常謝謝你，培根先生。

5. *Flight Attendant*

Miss Lin passes the examination required of applicants for flight attendants for the Transpacific Airlines Company. She has been granted an interview with Mr. Benson, the personnel manager of the Taipei branch office.

(*B* : *Mr. Benson* *L* : *Miss Lin*)

B : Please have a seat.

L : Thank you.

B : So you would like to become a flight attendant. What made you decide on this type of occupation?

L : I like traveling very much and I enjoy working with people.

B : Have you ever been abroad?

L : Yes. I was an exchange student when I was in high school. I stayed in California for about ten months.

B : Would you describe your character briefly?

L : No problem. I think I'm a tactful and amiable person. I like to be with a group of people, and I also think that no man is an island. Therefore, I like to listen to and communicate with others.

5. 空服員

林小姐通過了「泛太平洋航空公司」的空服員考試。
她獲准和台北分公司的人事經理班森先生面談。

（B：班森先生　L：林小姐）

班　森：請坐。

林小姐：謝謝。

班　森：妳想當空服員，是什麼使妳決定選擇這個職業？

林小姐：我很喜歡旅行，也喜歡和人們一起工作。

班　森：妳曾經出過國嗎？

林小姐：是的，我高中時當過交換學生，在加州待了大約十
　　　　個月。

班　森：妳可以簡短地描述一下妳的個性嗎？

林小姐：沒問題。我覺得我是個圓滑而且和藹可親的人。我喜
　　　　歡和一群人在一起，而且我也認為沒有人是一座孤島。
　　　　所以，我喜歡傾聽還有與他人溝通。

B : I see. Do you realize, Miss Lin, that being a flight attendant is not an easy job? You must deal with many kinds of people and sometimes you would have to work long hours.

L : Yes, I know that.

B : How's your health condition? Did you ever suffer any serious disease?

L : No. I'm always a very healthy person. I have no history of hospitalization.

B : Have you had any nursing experience? How about taking care of children? Have you ever been a baby-sitter?

L : Yes. My brother is 8 years younger than I, and my mother always wanted me to take care of him. My brother and I are very close, so I'm confident that I'm a great baby-sitter.

B : Do you like to cook?

L : Yes, cooking is my hobby. I have taken lessons in French cooking.

B : Well, you wouldn't be expected to cook, but as you know, you will have to serve meals. I think you are acquainted with our salary system and working conditions. Do you have any questions?

L : How about your training program? Would we trained here in Taiwan?

班　森：原來如此。林小姐，妳知道當一個空服員不是件輕鬆
　　　　的工作嗎？妳必須和很多種人接觸，而且有時候還得
　　　　長時間工作。

林小姐：是的，我知道。

班　森：妳的健康狀況如何？妳曾經罹患任何重大疾病嗎？

林小姐：沒有。我一向是個很健康的人。我沒有任何住院的經
　　　　歷。

班　森：妳有任何看護經驗嗎？例如照顧小孩？妳曾經當過臨
　　　　時褓母嗎？

林小姐：有的。我弟弟小我八歲，我媽總是要我照顧他。我弟
　　　　弟和我很親，所以我確信自己是個出色的臨時褓母。

班　森：妳喜歡烹飪嗎？
林小姐：喜歡，烹飪是我的嗜好，我學過烹飪法國菜。

班　森：好，妳不必做菜，但是正如妳所知，妳必須供應餐點。
　　　　我想妳對於我們的薪資制度和工作情況都非常了解。
　　　　妳有任何問題嗎？

林小姐：那貴公司的訓練課程呢？我們就在台灣這裡受訓嗎？

B : Yes, our training facilities are located in Taoyuan City. You would be trained there for six weeks. If you are hired, you would be expected to report for training on the 21st of next month. Would that be convenient for you?

L : Yes, fine.

B : We are considering several other applicants and we will make our decision by the end of next week. We will call you regardless of whether you are hired or not. Thank you for coming, Miss Lin. It was nice talking to you.

L : Thank you, Mr. Benson.

Far Eastern Air Transport seeks flight attendants and ground crew.

Requirements:

    *female

    *less than 28 years old

    *adept in Chinese, Taiwanese and English

    *TOEIC score of no less than 550

班　森：是的，我們的訓練設備位於桃園市。妳要在那裡受訓六週。如果妳被錄取，下個月二十一號就要來報到受訓。妳方便嗎？

林小姐：是的，沒問題。

班　森：我們還在考慮其他幾位應徵者，我們會在下星期做出決定。不論妳是否錄取，我們都會打電話給妳。謝謝妳過來面試，林小姐，和妳談話很愉快。

林小姐：謝謝你，班森先生。

6. Tour Guide

Huang Ke Ming is graduating from the English Department of Fu Jen University, and applying for work with a travel agency which specializes in package tours overseas for Chinese groups. He is being interviewed by Mr. Freeman, English consultant for the agency.

(*F*: *Mr. Freeman* *H* : *Huang Ke Ming*)

F : Hello, Mr. Huang. Won't you sit down?

H : Thank you.

F : Now, you probably know that this interview is mostly to test your presence of mind in English, so just relax, and let's chat, shall we?

H : All right.

F : Let's start with your personal history. Do you have any work experience?

H : Yes, when I was in college, I tutored a high school student in English. I've done this job for two years now.

6. 導 遊

> 黃克明即將從輔大英語系畢業,他向一個專門包辦中國團體海外旅遊的旅行社應徵工作。他正在和旅行社的英文顧問福瑞曼先生面談。

(**F**:福瑞曼先生 **H**:黃克明)

福瑞曼:嗨,黃先生,請坐。

黃克明:謝謝。

福瑞曼:現在,你大概知道這個面試主要是用英文來測試你夠不夠鎮定,所以只管放輕鬆,我們聊聊,好嗎?

黃克明:好。

福瑞曼:我們從你的個人經歷開始吧。你有任何工作經驗嗎?

黃克明:有的,當我還在唸大學時,我擔任一位高中生的英文家教。我做那份工作至今已有兩年了。

F : Have you ever led a group of people or had any other similar experience?

H : Mm. Actually, when I was a freshman in college, I served as a conductor in the China Youth Corps during summer vacation. My classmates and I led a group of twenty children. We went to climb mountains and did some recreational activities. To me, that was a really precious experience.

F : OK. Then what got you interested in working for a travel agency?

H : Well, that's a long story, actually. Ever since I was little, I've been interested in foreign countries, especially their cultures and antiquities. I majored in English in college so that I'd be able to understand those cultures better. I'm especially interested in the United States. Are you American?

F : No, I'm Canadian, actually.

H : Oh, sorry. I think I just put my foot in my mouth!

F : Oh, that's all right. I'm getting used to it.

H : Well, anyway, excuse me for getting off the subject. As I said, I'm very interested in foreign countries, especially those in the West, so when I began thinking about getting a job, a travel agency seemed the logical choice. I'd like to be an overseas tour guide, actually.

福瑞曼：　你是否曾經帶領一群人，或是有沒有其他類似的經驗？

黃克明：　嗯，事實上，當我大一時，我曾在暑假期間擔任救國團的嚮導。我和我同學帶領一群小朋友，他們有二十個人。我們去爬山和做一些娛樂活動。對我而言，那真的是很珍貴的經驗。

福瑞曼：　好的。是什麼使你對在旅行社工作感興趣？

黃克明：　嗯，其實說來話長。我從小就對外國很感興趣，尤其是它們的文化和古蹟。我大學時主修英文，所以比較能夠了解那些文化。我對美國特別感興趣。你是美國人嗎？

福瑞曼：　不，實際上我是加拿大人。

黃克明：　哦，抱歉。我想我說錯話了！

福瑞曼：　喔，沒關係，我習慣了。

黃克明：　嗯，無論如何，原諒我離開主題。就像我剛說的，我對外國很感興趣，尤其是那些西方國家，所以當我開始考慮找工作時，旅行社似乎就是個合理的選擇。事實上，我想當個海外導遊。

F : There's a good chance of that if you come to work for this company. Not right away, of course, but in a few years, after people learn something about the way the business runs, a lot of them go overseas with a group, or go beforehand to set up hotel arrangements and such.

H : That would be interesting. I'd like to be a good tour guide, and help people really enjoy their trip.
(*A buzzer sounds on Mr. Freeman's desk.*)

F : Ah, that's Mr. Wang. He is ready to give you your Chinese interview. His room is two doors down and to the right. I've enjoyed talking with you.

H : Thank you very much.

F : Thank you for coming.

> Global travel agency needs experienced
> bilingual guide. Good people skills and
> Spanish essential, English speaking helpful.
> Send resume and samples of writing
> (English and Spanish) to:
> Personnel Dept.
> Petroleum Magazine
> P.O. Box 7820
> Tulsa, Ok 74102

福瑞曼： 如果你替本公司工作，你就會有很好的機會。當然不是馬上，但是過幾年，等你們對營業情況比較了解一點之後，很多人就會跟著旅行團到國外去，或是先去訂旅館等等。

黃克明： 那一定很有意思。我想當一個好導遊，並幫助人們真正地享受旅遊。

（福瑞曼先生桌上的電鈴響了。）

福瑞曼： 啊，那是王先生，他準備和你用中文面談。他的房間在靠右邊兩間。和你談話很愉快。

黃克明： 非常謝謝你。

福瑞曼： 謝謝你來面試。

7. *Nurse*

> Miss Chiang had been working as a nurse in a hospital in Taiwan. She found an opening in the Help Wanted section of The New York Times.
>
> Nurses! We need your skills. Part time or full time. Top pay, good benefits. Experience desirable. Write:
>
> Municipal Hospital
> New York, NY 46254
>
> Now the Director of Nursing, Mrs. Nelson, is interviewing her.

(*N* : *Mrs. Nelson* *C*: *Miss Chiang*)

N : You are Miss Chiang?

C : That's right.

N : Did you bring the papers that will verify your qualifications?

C : Yes, here they are.

N : (*Looking over her file*) Do you have a United States R.N. license?

C : No, as I have just arrived here, I haven't had a chance to take the exam.

7. 護 士

江小姐一直在台灣的醫院當護士。她在「紐約時報」
的求職欄發現一個工作機會。

護士！我們需要妳的技術。

兼差或全職，高薪，福利好，

有經驗佳。来信請寄：

市立醫院

紐約，NY 46254

現在她正和護理長尼爾森女士面談。

（ *N*：尼爾森女士 *C*：江小姐 ）

尼爾森： 妳是江小姐？

江小姐： 是的。

尼爾森： 妳帶了資格證明文件嗎？

江小姐： 帶了，在這裡。

尼爾森： （看她的資料）妳有美國的護士執照嗎？

江小姐： 沒有，因為我才剛到這裡，還沒有機會去考試。

N : I see. Well, how about your nursing education in Taiwan?

C : I learned nursing through theory and practice for four years at the Department of Nursing in Taiwan University. And I got an R.N. license in 2001, the year of my graduation.

N : Did you have any nursing experience in a hospital before coming to the States?

C : Yes, I worked at the Veteran's Hospital in Taipei.

N : Did you work there long?

C : A little over two years.

N : What are the wards in which you have worked?

C : I have worked in a surgical ward.

N : If you are hired by this hospital, what ward would you like to work in?

C : If possible, I'd like you to try me in the medical ward.

N : As you know, this hospital is located in the center of the city. So we're always very busy and need to work overtime very often. Can you accept this kind of work environment?

C : I'll try my best to adjust myself to this hospital. Additionally, when you need me, I'm willing to work overtime.

尼爾森： 原來如此，那麼，妳在台灣受過哪些護理教育呢？

江小姐： 我在台大護理系學了四年的護理理論和實際，並在 2001 年，也就是我畢業那年，拿到護士執照。

尼爾森： 妳到美國之前，有任何在醫院當護士的經驗嗎？

江小姐： 有，我在台北的榮民總醫院工作過。

尼爾森： 妳在那裡做了很久嗎？

江小姐： 兩年多。

尼爾森： 妳在什麼病房工作？

江小姐： 我在外科病房工作。

尼爾森： 如果妳被這家醫院錄用，妳想在什麼病房工作？

江小姐： 如果可能的話，我希望您能讓我在內科病房試做。

尼爾森： 正如妳所知，這家醫院是位於市中心。所以我們一向非常忙碌，而且很常加班。妳能接受這種工作環境嗎？

江小姐： 我會盡力配合這家醫院。此外，當您需要我時，我很樂意加班。

N : Why have you decided to work in the U.S.A? You may spend several months getting accustomed to living in New York.

C : Well, my family emigrated to the U.S.A one year ago. If I get this job, then I'll moved to New York and live with them.

N : All right. We'll let you know within five days. Thank you for coming by.

C : Thank you. I'll look forward to hearing from you.

One Nurse & one Doctor in Dermatology
Presentable appearance required as they
will be in a cosmetic hospital associated
with beauty and skin care.

Age: 23-30.
Experience: minimum 3 years.
Salary: US$800 & US$1000 gross.
More information: www.cosmetics.org

尼爾森： 妳為什麼決定要在美國工作？妳可能要花幾個月的時
　　　　 間來適應在紐約的生活。

江小姐： 嗯，我的家人在一年前就移民到美國了。如果我得到
　　　　 這份工作，那我就可以搬到紐約和他們一起住了。

尼爾森： 好，五天之內我們會讓妳知道。謝謝妳來。

江小姐： 謝謝，我期待你們的消息。

8. *Computer Game Programmer*

> Super PK Company needs a new, young computer game program designer. Mr. Wu's professor at National Taiwan University, Mr. Wang, encouraged him to apply for the position available. Mr. Wu has come for an interview with Mr. Laurence.

(*L* : *Mr. Laurence* *W* : *Mr. Wu*)

L : Good morning. You're Mr. Wu?

W : Yes, that's right.

L : Have a seat, please.

W : Thank you, Mr. Lorence.

L : What did you major in?

W : Electrical engineering.

L : What is it that interests you about computer games?

W : There are lots of things, of course, but the most important one is the challenge, I think. I have loved computer games since my childhood. I think that computer games not only provide recreation, but also improve our reflexes.

8. 電玩程式設計師

> 「超級 PK 公司」需要一位年輕的新任電玩程式設計師。吳先生在台大時的教授，王先生，鼓勵他去應徵這個職位。吳先生前來和羅倫斯先生面談。

（*L*：羅倫斯先生　*W*：吳先生）

羅倫斯： 早安，你是吳先生嗎？

吳先生： 是的，沒錯。

羅倫斯： 請坐。

吳先生： 謝謝你，羅倫斯先生。

羅倫斯： 你主修什麼？

吳先生： 電機工程。

羅倫斯： 你對電玩的哪一方面感興趣？

吳先生： 當然，我對很多部分都感興趣，但是我想，最主要的，是有挑戰性。我從小就喜歡電玩。我認為電玩不但提供娛樂，它還可以增進我們的反應速度。

L : What's your primary interest in this job?

W : To be frank, I'm very interested in designing the barriers of computer games.

L : What made you pick this company?

W : Well, your company was just established two years ago, and I suppose that there will be more chances to advance. Moreover, my college professor, Mr. Wang is acquainted with the president of this company, and he told me that the president is an open-minded person. And I hope to follow this kind of leader.

L : Do you have any certificates?

W : Yes, I just got a professional engineering license in the United States.

L : You may have chances to communicate with foreign engineers in our company. Can you deal with such situations?

W : Of course I can. My TOEIC score was about 750. I believe I can deal with general situations and communicate with foreign engineers in English.

L : Is there anything you would like to know about the job?

W : Yes. What is your starting salary, and what sort of fringe benefits does the job offer?

羅倫斯： 那麼你主要是對這份工作的哪個部分感興趣？

吳先生： 坦白說，我對於設計電玩遊戲的關卡最有興趣。

羅倫斯： 什麼原因使你選擇本公司？

吳先生： 嗯，貴公司兩年前才創立，所以我想這裡會有比較多
的陞遷機會。此外，我的大學教授，王先生，他認識
這家公司的總裁，他告訴我說，總裁是個能接受新思
想的人。而我希望能跟隨這樣的領導者。

羅倫斯： 你有任何證照嗎？

吳先生： 有，我剛取得美國的專業工程師執照。

羅倫斯： 在本公司，你可能會有機會要和外國工程師溝通。你
能應付這種狀況嗎？

吳先生： 我當然可以。我的多益測驗成績約為 750 分。我相信
我能用英語處理一般情況，並和外國工程師溝通。

羅倫斯： 關於這份工作，你還有什麼想知道的？

吳先生： 有的。起薪是多少，以及這份工作有提供什麼特別的
福利嗎？

L : The starting salary for an engineer is 35,000 dollars a month, and raises would be given after the first six months according to your ability. There are semiannual bonuses, three weeks paid vacation a year, and health insurance.

L : Well, Mr. Wu. I've enjoyed talking with you, but I have another appointment in just a few minutes. Thank you very much for coming today.

W : Thank you, Mr. Laurence.

L : You'll be hearing a definite answer from us within a week. Good-bye.

W : Good-bye.

Engineer, Full Time.

Requirements
1. Degree in Electrical Engineering.
2. At least 2 years experience in developing embedded systems.
3. Ability to read and understand and apply technical documents.
4. Ability to stay and work for at least 5 years.

Interested candidates should apply with a comprehensive resume stating education and work history to: abey@electric.net

羅倫斯： 工程師的起薪是每個月三萬五千元，六個月後，依能
力調薪。每半年有獎金，每年有三個星期的給薪假期
和健保。

羅倫斯： 嗯，吳先生，很高興和你談話，但是我再過幾分鐘後
還有約會。非常謝謝你今天來面試。

吳先生： 謝謝您，羅倫斯先生。

羅倫斯： 我們會在一星期內給你明確的答覆。再見。

吳先生： 再見。

第③篇▶簽證面面觀

Visa English

1. *About Yourself* 關於自己

簽證官 ： What is your name, please?
　　　　請問你叫什麼名字？

申請者 ： My name is Lee Yu Hsin, sir (ma'am).
　　　　我叫李又新，先生（女士）。

簽證官 ： When were you born?
　　　　你是什麼時候出生的？

申請者 ： I was born on February 18th, 1983.
　　　　我生於 1983 年 2 月 18 日。

簽證官 ： Where were you born?
　　　　你是在哪裡出生的？

申請者 ： I was born in Taipei, sir (ma'am).
　　　　我出生於台北，先生（女士）。

簽證官 ： What are you doing now?
　　　　你現在從事什麼行業？

申請者 ： I am a senior at Chengchi University now.
　　　　我現在是政大四年級的學生。

　　　　I am working for a foreign trading company as an administrative assistant.
　　　　我現在在外貿公司當行政助理。

　　　　I have been working as a government official.
　　　　我一直在當公務員。

簽證官： Are you married?
　　　　 你結婚了嗎？

申請者： No. I'm single.
　　　　 沒有。我單身。

　　　　 Yes, I'm married.
　　　　 是的，我已婚。

簽證官： Do you want your wife to go with you?
　　　　 你要你太太和你一起去嗎？

申請者： No, that will cost a lot of money. The price level
　　　　 in the U.S. is too high.
　　　　 不行，那會花很多錢。美國的物價水準太高了。

　　　　 No, my wife has her own job in Taiwan. And I
　　　　 promised her that I'll come back soon after I get
　　　　 my Ph.D.
　　　　 不，我太太在台灣有自己的工作。而且我向她保證，
　　　　 我一拿到博士學位，馬上就會回國。

簽證官： Do you have any relatives or friends in the States?
　　　　 你在美國有任何親戚或朋友嗎？

申請者： No, I don't.
　　　　 不，我沒有。

　　　　 Yes, my brother, who runs a Chinese restaurant, is
　　　　 in New York.
　　　　 有，我哥哥在紐約開中國餐館。

簽證官： Are you religious?
你有宗教信仰嗎？

申請者： Yes, I am a Christian.
有，我是個基督徒。

Yes, I am a Buddhist.
有，我是個佛教徒。

No. I am an atheist.
沒有。我是無神論者。

簽證官： Have you served in the army?
你當過兵嗎？

申請者： Yes, I have.
是，我當過。

No, I was exempted from military service because
I'm very shortsighted.
沒有，我免服兵役。因為我近視很深。

簽證官： Have you ever applied for a visa before?
你以前曾經申請過簽證嗎？

申請者： No, sir. I haven't.
沒有，先生，我沒申請過。

No, this is the first time. 沒有，這是第一次。

Yes, I have twice.
有，我申請過兩次。

簽證官 ： What do your parents think of your studying abroad?
你父母對你要出國留學有什麼看法？

申請者 ： They agree with me.
他們都贊成。

My father studied in the U.S., too. He always gives
me encouragement.
我父親以前也在美國唸過書。他一直鼓勵我。

2. *Educational Background* 學　歷

簽證官 : What school did you graduate from?
你是什麼學校畢業的？

申請者 : I graduated from National Sun Yat-sen University.
我畢業於國立中山大學。

I am attending National Taiwan University.
我目前還在台大唸書。

簽證官 : What year are you in?
你唸幾年級？

申請者 : I am a freshman (sophomore/junior/senior).
我唸一年級（二年級/三年級/四年級）。

簽證官 : What is your major?
你主修什麼？

申請者 : I am majoring in public administration.
我主修公共行政。

I am specialized in law.
我專攻法律。

My major is mechanical engineering.
我主修機械工程。

簽證官： Tell me something about your educational
background.
告訴我你的學歷。

申請者： I completed elementary, junior and senior high school
in Tungkang, Pingtung County. And then I entered
Taiwan University in Taipei, where I'm studying now.
我在屏東東港唸完小學、國中和高中，然後在台北唸台灣大
學，也就是我現在唸的學校。

簽證官： How long has it been since you graduated from
college?
你從大學畢業多久了？

申請者： I graduated from college two years ago.
我兩年前從大學畢業。

簽證官： When did you graduate from college?
你何時從大學畢業的？

申請者： I graduated from college in 2001.
我在二〇〇一年時，從大學畢業。

3. *Grades* 成 績

簽證官： How were your grades in college?

你大學時成績如何？

申請者： My GPA was 3.0. In my freshman and sophomore years I didn't know exactly what I wanted to study, and I didn't work very hard. Then all of a sudden in my junior year, I realized that I wasn't going anywhere that way, and if I didn't get serious it would be too late pretty soon, so I started to work harder. My grades got better after that.

我的學業成績總平均是 3.0。在大一和大二時，我不清楚自己到底想唸什麼，所以不用功。後來在大三那年，我突然了解到，那樣我會毫無進展，而且如果我再不認真，馬上就會太遲了，所以我開始更加努力用功。我的成績也在那之後開始好轉。

I graduated with a GPA of 3.5. The first two years were general studies rather than major classes, and I didn't find them very interesting. But from my junior year I was able to choose my own courses, and I got really interested in what I was studying.

我畢業的學業成績總平均是 3.5。頭兩年是一般課程，而不是主修課程，所以我不是很感興趣。但是從大三開始，我可以自己選課，因此也對我唸的東西真正感到有興趣。

申請者：My grades weren't very good. I spent almost all my time on club activities, and missed a lot of classes. But I think that I also learned a lot of things from club activities that are not taught in class.

我的成績不是很好，我幾乎把所有的時間都花在社團活動上，所以缺了很多堂課。但是我認為，我也從社團活動中，學到很多課堂上沒有教授的知識。

簽證官：What will you do your thesis for your Ph.D. on?
你的博士論文打算做什麼？
= Tell me what are you doing your thesis on and something about your paper.
請告訴我你的畢業論文是做什麼，還有一些相關內容。

申請者：My Ph.D. thesis is about how to rally Taiwan's economical development. I addressed two main issues. First, we need to develop more professional managers and strengthen our marketing ability. Second, we must improve our investment environment. Then we can attract more foreign capital. Those are the bare bones of my thesis.

我的博士論文是關於如何重振台灣的經濟發展。我提出了兩個主要的方向。首先，我們必須培養更多專業經理人，以強化我們的行銷能力。第二，我們必須改善投資環境，才能吸引更多外資。那就是我的畢業論文架構。

簽證官： You got a low score in calculus. Why?

你的微積分成績不高，爲什麼？

申請者： I haven't been good at math since I was a junior high school student. But I plan to study history in the U.S.A., so I don't think I need to worry about my math scores anymore.

我從國中開始就不擅長數學。但我打算在美國攻讀歷史，所以我覺得我再也不必擔心我的數學成績了。

Well, our calculus professor had just graduated from Columbia University at that time, and he changed his teaching methods very often. We didn't know how to get used to his teaching, so the average score of my class was just 70.

嗯，我們的微積分教授當時剛從哥倫比亞大學畢業，而且他常常改變教學方式。我們不知道該如何適應他的教法，所以全班的平均分數只有七十分。

4. Motivation 動 機

簽證官： What is your purpose in applying for a visa?
你申請簽證的目的是什麼？

申請者： I want to study public administration at Columbia University.
我想到哥倫比亞大學唸公共行政。

I want to further my education in the U.S. and use an MBA as a springboard for career improvement.
我想到美國進修，並以MBA（企管碩士）作爲事業進展的跳板。

簽證官： Why do you want to study in the U.S.?
你爲什麼想在美國唸書？

申請者： Because I think the study of business administration is most advanced in the U.S.
因爲我認爲美國的企管研究是最先進的。

Because M.I.T. has an excellent program in electrical engineering, my major. I want to continue my education there.
因爲M.I.T.（麻省理工學院）在我主修的電機工程學方面有很好的課程，我想在那裡繼續受教育。

簽證官： What do you plan to do after graduation?
你畢業後，計畫要做什麼？

申請者： I hope to teach students in Taiwan.
我希望在台灣教書。

I would like to become a professor in Taiwan after studying further in the U.S.
在美國深造後，我想回台灣當教授。

I expect to return to the company where I am working now. 我希望回到我目前工作的公司。

簽證官： You are going to study instead of emigrating, is that true? 你是去唸書而不是移民，這是真的嗎？

申請者： Yes, I do not intend to move to the U.S. I just want to study further in a more advanced country.
是的，我不打算搬到美國。我只是想到一個比較先進的國家進修。

簽證官： Since your graduation, many years have passed. Do you have any particular reason to study in the States now?
你已經畢業很多年了，現在到美國唸書，有什麼特別原因嗎？

申請者： Actually, I am earning a fairly good salary here. But I have never been satisfied with my present knowledge and want to learn new things. If I'm successful there, I'll have a chance to be the director of our company.
事實上，我目前在這裡的薪水相當不錯，但是我從來不滿於我現有的知識，而且想學習新的東西；如果我在那裡唸得好，就有機會成為我們公司的主任。

申請者： I couldn't afford the expense of studying in the States before. But I have saved enough money since my graduation from college.

我以前負擔不起到美國讀書的費用，但是從大學畢業到現在，我已經存夠了錢。

簽證官： You've got a really good job in Taiwan. Why do you still want to study abroad?

你在台灣已經有很好的工作。為什麼還要到國外唸書？

申請者： I think if I want to keep myself at the top of the business field forever, then I need to learn more and more. Your country is the leader in electrical engineering, so I think I can acquire professional knowledge there. After that, I plan to go back to Taiwan, and to found my own electronics company.

我認為如果我想讓自己永遠保持在商業界的頂尖，那麼我需要再多學一些東西。而貴國是電機工程方面的先驅，所以我想我可以在那裡學到專業的知識。學成之後，我打算回台灣，並創立自己的電子公司。

5. *About University* 學 校

簽證官 : What college are you going to?
你要唸什麼大學？

申請者 : I am going to Boston University in Massachusetts.
我要去唸麻薩諸塞州的波士頓大學。

簽證官 : Why do you want to study at the University of Minnesota?
你為什麼想唸明尼蘇達大學？

申請者 : Because of it's academic reputation. And it has an excellent sociology program, my major.
因為它的學術聲譽。而且它有非常出色的社會學課程，那是我的主修科目。

Because my professor encouraged me to study there and I am supposed to get a scholarship from the university.
因為我的教授鼓勵我到那裡進修，而且我應該可以拿到那所大學的獎學金。

簽證官 : What kind of degree do you plan to get?
你打算拿什麼學位？

申請者 : I want to receive a bachelor's degree and next a master's.
我想拿一個學士學位，然後再拿一個碩士學位。

I'm going to get a doctoral degree. 我要拿博士學位。

簽證官 ： How long do you plan to take to get your Ph.D.?
你打算花多久的時間拿到博士學位？

申請者 ： I sincerely hope that I can get my Ph.D. in three years, because my current company only promised to give me financial aid for three years.
我強烈希望可以在三年內拿到博士學位，因為我目前的公司只承諾要給我三年的經濟援助。

I plan to earn it as soon as possible. My parents are not young anymore. They need someone to take care of them and stay with them.
我打算儘快拿到博士學位。我的父母已經不再年輕了，他們需要有人來照顧和陪伴。

簽證官 ： Please give me three reasons why you selected King's College.
你為什麼選擇國王學院，請給我三個理由。

申請者 ： Well, first, I'm very interested in the history of England, and King's College was founded in 1441. It has a long history. Second, my major subject is medicine, and I think I can get a good education there. Besides, I've been to the King's College, and it is a really beautiful college.
嗯，首先，我對英國的歷史很有興趣，而國王學院創立於 1441 年，它的歷史很悠久。第二，我主修藥理學，我認為我可以在那裡得到良好的教育。此外，我曾經去過國王學院，而那真是一所美麗的大學。

簽證官： What are you going to major in?
你要主修什麼？

申請者： I'm going to major in English literature.
我要主修英國文學。

I'm going to study architecture.　我要唸建築。

簽證官： What will you study in America?
你要到美國唸什麼？

申請者： I'm going to study modern art.
我要去唸現代藝術。

I'll go to Harvard University and study in its law
school.　我要到哈佛大學唸法學院。

簽證官： In what aspect of your major will you specialize?
你將要唸你主修的哪個部分？

申請者： I majored in history when I was in National Taiwan
University, and I plan to study European history
further in French.
我在台大時是主修歷史，而我打算到法國進修歐洲史。

簽證官： Why do you want to change your major?
你為什麼要改變你的主修科目？

申請者： My major is English literature but my mind isn't
liberal arts-oriented, I guess.　I have been interested
in architecture since I was a sophomore.
我主修英國文學，但是我想我的心性並不適合唸文科。
從大二開始，我就一直對建築有興趣。

申請者 : I majored in history but I've wanted to be involved in writing ever since I was little.
我主修歷史，但我從小就一直想從事寫作。

簽證官 : Have you received any kind of scholarship?
你有任何一種獎學金嗎？

申請者 : No, I haven't.
不，我沒有。

Yes, I have received a full scholarship.
有，我有全額獎學金。

Yes, I am supposed to get a scholarship, which will enable me to study there for one year.
有，我應該會拿到獎學金，那夠我在那裡唸一年。

6. *English Ability* 英文能力

簽證官： Do you think your English is good enough for work at an American college?

你認爲你的英文足以在美國唸大學嗎？

申請者： Yes, I think so. I've studied English very hard in order to be well prepared.

是的，我想可以。我很努力學英文，以做好充分的準備。

I think so, but I am afraid my English is a little weak. So I intend to take a language course before enrolling in graduate school.

我想可以，但是我怕我的英文能力稍嫌薄弱，所以我打算在進研究所之前，先上語言課程。

Yes, I have wanted to study abroad for a long time, so I spend much time improving my English ability.

是的，我很久以前就想出國留學，所以我花很多時間來增進自己的英文能力。

No, but I'll solve my language problem by taking a language course in the university.

不，但是我會在大學選讀語言課程，來解決我的問題。

簽證官： Have you taken the TOEFL test?

你參加過托福考試了嗎？

申請者： Yes, I have. I scored 600.

有，我參加了，我得 600 分。

申請者： Yes, I received a score of 570 on TOEFL test.

有，我托福考試得 570 分。

I haven't had time to take the TOEFL yet because I just recently decided to study in the States. But I'm confident of my English speaking and reading.

我還沒有時間去考托福，因為我是最近才決定到美國唸書。但我對於自己的英文說讀能力很有信心。

簽證官： How many points did you get on your TOEFL test?
= What was your TOEFL score?

你托福考試得幾分？

申請者： I got 600 points on it.

我得到 600 分。

I got 230 points on the computer-based test.

我在托福電腦測驗中拿到 230 分。

7. Financial Support 財 力

簽證官： Who is going to support you while you are studying in the U.S.?
你在美國唸書的時候，誰會資助你？

=Who will provide you the money?
誰會提供你這筆資金？

=Where will you get money for the next few years?
往後幾年，你要從哪裡得到資金呢？

申請者： My father will pay for all my school expenses.
我父親會支付我全部的學費。

My elder brother working in L.A. will support me.
我哥哥在 L.A.（洛杉磯）工作，他會資助我。

It's at my own expense. I have more than enough to support myself for 2 years.
用我自己的錢，我的錢供我自己唸兩年綽綽有餘。

簽證官： Who will finance your tuition and other expenses?
誰會資助你學雜費？

申請者： I am supposed to get a full scholarship.
我應該會拿到一個全額的獎學金。

The government will take full responsibility.
政府會全額負擔。

My mother will be my sponsor during my stay in the U.S.A.
我媽媽會贊助我留美期間的費用。

簽證官： What's your relationship with your sponsor?
你和你的贊助人是什麼關係？

申請者： He is my father. 他是我父親。

My uncle. 我叔叔。

簽證官： What is he doing in the U.S.?
他在美國是做什麼的？

Where will your sponsor get the funds from?
你的贊助人從哪裡拿到這些資金？

申請者： He is a dentist in Los Angeles. 他在洛杉磯當牙醫。

He is now working at Ford Motors as a mechanic.
他目前在福特汽車公司當技師。

He runs a supermarket in L.A.
他在洛杉磯經營超級市場。

My father has worked as a government official for seven years, and he plans to use his savings to support me.
我父親當了七年的政府官員，他計劃用他的存款來資助我。

簽證官： How much is your parents' income per year?
你父母的年收入是多少？

申請者： I think it's about $2,000,000 NTD.
我想大概是新台幣兩百萬元。

They both retired from work several years ago. Now I'm depending on my brother's support, and his income is about $2,000,000 NTD.
他們在幾年前都退休了。我現在是靠我哥哥的資助，而他的年收入約為新台幣兩百萬元。

8. Length of Stay 停留時間

簽證官： How long do you plan to stay in the U.S.?
你計畫在美國待多久？

How long will you study in the U.S.A.?
你會在美國唸多久？

申請者： I suppose I will have to stay for about 3 years.
我想我大概得待個三年。

In order to receive a master's degree, I'll have to be
there for about two years.
為了拿碩士學位，我大約得在那裡待兩年。

I intend to stay at least five years.
我打算至少待五年。

I will stay there four years as stated on the I-20 form.
我會照 I-20 表上寫的，在美國待四年。

簽證官： Do you have strong personal relationships or
financial investment to ensure that you'll come
back to Taiwan?
你能以有力的人際關係或財務投資，來證明你會回台灣嗎？

申請者： Of course I do, sir. I'm planning to come back to
Taiwan after graduation and I hope to teach students
in Taiwan.
當然可以，先生。我打算畢業後就回台灣，我希望在台
灣教書。

申請者： Yes, and as soon as I finish I'll return to my country and look for a chance to apply what I've learned

可以，而且我一唸完就會回到我的國家，並希望能有機會應用所學。

I'll come back to my country after finishing my study in the states, because my uncle plans to let me be the sales manager of his company.

在美國唸完書之後，我會回到我的國家。因爲我叔叔打算讓我擔任他公司的業務經理。

Yes, of course. All of my family and friends live in Taiwan. Therefore, I'm very sure that after I graduate from grad school, I'll come back to Taiwan right away.

是的，當然可以。我所有的家人和朋友都住在台灣。因此，我很確定我從研究所畢業之後，一定會馬上回台灣。

Yes. I can assure you that I'll come back to my own country. Because the company which I'm serving now is giving me the chance to study further, I need to come back and reciprocate the favor.

可以。我能向你保證，我一定會回自己的國家。因爲我目前任職的公司給我這個進修的機會，所以我必須回來報答公司的恩惠。

9. Visit to the U.S 訪 美

簽證官： What is the purpose of your visit to the U.S.?
你訪美的目的是什麼？

申請者： I am going to visit my brother in New York.
我要到美國探望我在紐約的弟弟。

I am going on a business trip to New York.
我要到紐約出差。

I am going to attend a seminar (wedding/fair) in Chicago.
我要去參加一個在芝加哥舉辦的研討會（婚禮/博覽會）。

I am going on a sightseeing tour at the invitation of my daughter.
我女兒邀請我去觀光。

I plan to take a vacation in Florida.
我打算到佛羅里達州渡假。

I must go to Seattle to handle my grandfather's estate. 我要到西雅圖去處理我祖父的財產。

My company is sending me to assume the position of regional manager of the head office in Boston.
我們公司派我去擔任波士頓總公司的區域經理一職。

簽證官： Have you ever been to the U.S.?
你曾經去過美國嗎？

申請者： No. This is my first visit.
沒有，這是我第一次去。

申請者： Yes, I have been there once (twice / three times / many times).

有，我去過一次 (兩次/三次/很多次)。

I went there last year.

我去年去過。

No, I've been to the U.S. several times in my dreams, but not in reality.

沒有，我在夢裡去過美國很多次了，但沒有眞正到過美國。

簽證官： How long do you expect to stay in the U.S.?

你打算在美國待多久？

申請者： Just for three weeks.

只有三個禮拜。

For about a month or two.

大約會待一兩個月。

One month.

待一個月。

No more than two years, because my fiancée in Taiwan promised to wait for me for just two years.

不會超過兩年，因爲我在台灣的未婚妻只承諾等我兩年。

簽證官： Are you going to travel alone?

你要自己單獨前往嗎？

申請者： Yes, I have to go by myself.

是的，我得自己一個人去。

申請者： No, my friend sent me a letter of invitation for my wife and me.

不是，我朋友寫信來邀請我太太和我。

No, I'll go with my wife and my little boy. We're going to visit my parents. They emigrated to California last year.

不是，我要和我妻子還有小兒子一起去。我們將去探望我父母。他們去年移民到加州去。

簽證官： Do you have any relatives or friends in the States?

你在美國有任何親戚朋友嗎？

申請者： No, I don't. 不，我沒有。

Yes, my uncle has been there for 10 years.

有，我叔叔在那裡住了十年。

Yes, my son was assigned to the branch office in New York two years ago.

有，我兒子兩年前被派到紐約的分公司。

簽證官： Where is he working? 他在哪裡工作？

申請者： He is working for A&M Company in Los Angeles.

他在洛杉磯 A&M 公司工作。

He is a doctor now practicing medicine in San Francisco. 他現在在舊金山當醫生。

He is a government official at the foreign office.

他是外交部的政府官員。

簽證官：Who will pay for your travel expenses?
誰會支付你的旅費？

申請者：My friend invited me and he will do it.
我的朋友邀請我，所以他會付旅費。

My brother sent me a roundtrip ticket.
我哥哥給了我一張來回票。

My company will provide me with all the expenses.
我們公司會提供我所有的費用。

簽證官：What is your destination?
你的目的地是哪裡？

申請者：Los Angeles, California, sir.
加州洛杉磯，先生。

I am going to New York.
我要去紐約。

簽證官：Have you ever applied for a U.S. visa before?
你以前有沒有申請過美國簽證？

申請者：No, this is the first time.
沒有，這是第一次。

Yes, I have once.
有，我申請過一次。

10. *Emigration ·Getting a Job Abroad* 移民・海外求職

簽證官： What is the purpose of your visit to the U.S.?
你去美國的目的是什麼？

申請者： I am going as an immigrant.
我要移民。

I am going there to get a job.
我到那裡去工作。

簽證官： What type of business are you in now?
你現在從事什麼行業？

申請者： I am a tailor. I'm working for Levi Strauss & Co.,
which is so-called "Levi's". And it is a famous
brand of jeans.
我是個裁縫師。我在 Levi Strauss 公司工作，而那就
是俗稱的 "Levi's"。"Levi's" 是很有名的牛仔褲品牌。

I am a civil engineer. I've served seven years in the
Tong-Ling Building Corporation. Now the company
has decided to send me to Canada to work as a
senior engineer. So I plan to emigrate to Canada
and take this job.
我是個土木工程師。我在統領建設公司服務了七年。現
在公司決定要派我到加拿大，擔任高級工程師一職。所
以我打算移民加拿大，接受這份工作。

簽證官：Why do you want to get a job in the U.S.?
你爲什麼想在美國工作？

Why do you want to work abroad?
你爲什麼要到國外工作？

申請者：My uncle, who is running a gas station in L.A.,
wants me to come and help him.
我叔叔在洛杉磯經營加油站，要我去幫忙。

Originally, I worked for Taiwan Semiconductor
Manufacturing Company as an electrical engineer.
But this June, Intel company called me and said that
they are willing to give me higher pay and asked me
to work for them in U.S. After careful consideration,
I thought it was a good opportunity, so I decided to
accept this job offer.
我原本是在台積電當電機工程師。但今年六月，英特爾
公司打電話給我，它們要求我到美國替它們工作，而且
還願意出較高的薪資。經過仔細的考慮之後，我認爲這
是一個很好的機會，所以我決定接下這份工作。

All of my family emigrated to Canada last year. Since
then I've been searching for a suitable job, and this
May, I got a job as a lawyer's assistant in Vancouver.
So I plan to take this job and join my family.
我的家人去年全都移民到加拿大了。從那時起，我就開
始找合適的工作，而今年五月，我找到了一份工作，那
是在溫哥華擔任律師助理。所以我打算接下這份工作，
並和我的家人團聚。

簽證官：Do you have any kind of license?
你有任何一種執照嗎？

申請者：Yes, I have a special operator's license for heavy equipment and also a driver's license.
有，我有特殊重裝備技師執照和駕照。

No, I don't have any certificate of qualification, but I'm preparing for the certified public accountant test now, and I'm confident that I can pass it next year.
沒有，我沒有任何證書，但我目前正在準備會計師執照的考試，而且我有自信，能在明年通過考試。

Yes, I have a commercial pilot license, and I've been working for Mainland Airlines for three years.
有，我有商務飛行員執照，而且我已經在大陸航空公司工作三年了。

簽證官：Do you have a job offer in the U.S.?
你在美國有工作機會嗎？

申請者：Yes, I do. This is a copy of my contract.
是的，我有。這是我的合約書影本。

I'm afraid I don't. But my uncle in San Francisco is making arrangements for my placement.
恐怕沒有，但是我在舊金山的叔叔正在替我安排工作。

簽證官 ： What type of work are you going to do in the U.S.?
你到美國要從事哪一類的工作？

申請者 ： I am going to work for A&M company in Chicago.
我要去替芝加哥的 A&M 公司工作。

I'm going to start up a tailor shop. I've rented a
storefront in Los Angeles.
我要去開一家裁縫店。我已經在洛杉磯租了一間店面。

I'm going to run a Chinese restaurant. I bought an
old restaurant in California last year, and I decided
to redecorate it. My own Chinese restaurant will
open in this March.
我要經營一家中國餐廳。我去年在加州買了一間老舊的
餐廳，我決定要重新裝潢它。我自己的中國餐廳將在今
年三月開張。

I want to work as an auto mechanic. It's my field.
我要去當汽車技工。那是我的專業領域。

簽證官 ： What is your contract period?
你的合約期限是多久？

申請者 ： Just one year, sir.
只有一年，先生。

It lasts two and a half years.
它持續兩年半。

簽證官： Who will pay for the travel expenses?
誰會支付旅費？

申請者： It's at my own expense. 用我自己的經費。

My employer, Mr. Miles, will pay for them.
我的雇主邁爾斯先生會付。

簽證官： What is your intended place of entry?
你打算從哪裡入境？

申請者： My intended place of entry is San Francisco
airport.
我打算從舊金山的機場入境。

簽證官： What particular things do you like in America?
你最喜歡美國的什麼？

申請者： I like the culture and climate there. I think people
in America are more open-minded, and there are
several different kinds of races. I'm interested in
living with people from all over the world. Besides,
its climate are cooler and drier. I think I can get
used to such an environment very soon.
我喜歡那裡的文化和氣候。我認為美國人的思想比較開
明，而且那裡有好幾個不同的種族。我對於和來自世界
各地的人住在一起很有興趣。此外，那邊的氣候比較涼
爽和乾燥。我覺得我很快就能適應這種環境。

申請者： Well, I enjoy the space in U.S. the most. Everyone possesses his own room, and people don't have to live closely to each other. In addition, without so much people and cars, I think the air must be much cleaner.

嗯，我最喜歡的是美國開闊的空間。每個人都擁有自己的空間，而且人們不必住在離彼此很近的地方。此外，少了這麼多的人口和車輛，我想空氣一定會更加清新。

簽證官： Do you want to go to Australia because you are not successful in Taiwan?

你要到澳洲，是因為你在台灣過得不好嗎？

申請者： Of course not. My work experience can prove that I'm an outstanding mechanical engineer. I plan to emigrate to Australia because of my parents. They are getting older, so I hope they can settle down in an unpolluted place.

當然不是。我的工作經驗可以證明，我是個傑出的機械工程師。我打算移民到澳洲，是為了我父母。他們正逐漸年老，所以我希望他們能定居在沒有污染的地方。

No, I just want to change my living environment. I think I can learn more new things in a brand-new location.

不是，我只是想轉換一下生活環境。我覺得在一個全新的地方，可以學到更多新的東西。

第④篇 ▶ 留學簽證實況會話

Interview for Studying Abroad

留學簽證面談訣竅

第 1 章　美國留學簽證

　　美國的簽證官最擔心台灣學生藉故唸書，然後就非法居留在美國。因此申辦美國留學簽證時，務必要攜帶 I-20 和其他相關證明文件。I-20 是美國學校提供自費留學生申請簽證（F-1 Visa）時的入學證明文件，也有人稱之為「入學許可」。自費留學生通常會在四月份前後，收到美國學校發出的入學許可。一般而言，若有美國大學正式核發的 I-20，則申請簽證失敗的機率並不高。此外，在和簽證官面談時，最重要的，就是讓他們相信，你只是暫時出國唸書充電而已，絕對不會長期居留，而且要對自己的未來有十分明確的交代，像是到美國要唸什麼，唸完課程以後的計劃等。

　　要讓簽證官相信你沒有移民企圖的話，必須要表明台灣對你而言，是具有充分的約束力的。通常，簽證官會考慮申請人的職業、家庭以及財務狀況。而「約束力」是指每個人生活中，各種能使他和自己居住的地方緊緊相連的條件，如財產、職業、社交等，而對於沒有這種社會關係的年輕人，簽證官會考量申請人的特殊意向、家庭關係，和教育情況（是否還在求學階段）、學校成績、長期計劃，以及在台灣的發展等。代表充分約束力的條件，往往是因人而異的。一般較具有說服力的說法如下：

　　1. 在台灣的工作前景看好，捨不得放棄。
　　2. 親戚朋友都在台灣，且在台灣擁有不動產。

3. 赴美研讀的科系對台灣相當有幫助。

4. 有親屬在政府部門、科技業或教育界工作，且會在你畢業之後爲你安排好工作。

還有，簽證面談時，絕對要誠實回答簽證官的問題，例如：是否有親人在台灣，或是否申請過移民簽證。因爲所有的資料，都將經過電腦核對，所以如果申請人撒謊，將使得其所有證明文件的真實性受到質疑。

每年申請學生簽證的人爲數衆多，實際上被拒絕的機率也不算高，多半是因爲準備不足，或出國目標、理由不足，才會被退件。所以，能否取得簽證，並不是看單一理由，唯有事前做最充分的準備和模擬練習，才能增加取得簽證的機會。

美國留學簽證申請程序

事　　項	內　　　　　　　容
申請單位	美國在台協會 地址：台北市信義路三段 134 巷 7 號 電話：（02）2709-2000
受理時間	週一至週五，AM 7:30-11:30，台灣及美國國定假日除外
費　　用	非移民簽證爲每人新台幣三千六百元整 美國在台協會郵政劃撥帳號：19189005 戶名：美國銀行代收美國在台協會簽證手續費專戶 注意：每位申請人須繳交一張收據正本，該收據一年內有效。若簽證被拒，且欲重新申請者，須再繳一次手續費，並重填一張申請表

相 關 文 件	1.　一份用英文填妥的申請表格（DS-156），並貼上一 　張照片。表格上須註明台灣聯絡電話。本地地址可 　同時用英文及中文填寫，以利確認，但中文地址可 　選擇不寫。照片必須是 5 公分見方，全臉正面面對 　鏡頭，並於六個月內拍攝，頭頂至下巴需足 2.5 至 　3.5 公分之間，白色或灰白色背景，黑白或彩色照 　皆可 2.　十六歲到未滿四十六歲的男性申請人，須另外繳 　交以英文填妥的非移民簽證申請表補充說明 　（DS-157） 3.　F,J 及 M 簽證申請人，必須繳交一份用英文填妥 　的非移民簽證申請人聯絡資料及工作履歷表 　（DS-158） 4.　護照正本（請本人簽名，有效期間必須比預定居留 　期間多出六個月以上） 5.　曾經持有的護照。若是無法提出過去的護照，可提 　供一份歷年的出入境記錄，請向本地出入境管理局 　申請，地址是:台北市廣州街 15 號 　電話：23889393 6.　正面脫帽兩吋相片 1 張、財力證明 7.　若曾更改姓名，請攜帶一份戶籍謄本
護照發還	簽證及護照將透過超峰快遞服務，在申請提出後三到六 個工作日內，送交簽證申請人，費用爲新台幣一百五十 元整，同一地址一次可遞送四份護照。快遞申請表可在 非移民簽證科的等候大廳取得，護照遞送狀況可在網站 上查詢：http://www.express.com.tw/

美國留學簽證相關注意事項

1. 基本常識

⑴ 簽證有效期：指在那個日期內，必須進入美國，否則簽證失效。

⑵ 可停留效期：從入境之日起算，可在美國停留的期間，若申請停留時間較長，則需要多一點證明文件與費用。

⑶ 申根國家：歐洲有十個國家，包括法國、德國、西班牙、葡萄牙、荷蘭、比利時、盧森堡、奧地利、義大利、希臘，只要申請其中任何一國的簽證，就可以進出其他九個國家，但是要注意，進出時如果要到其他非申根國家，還是需要申請簽證。一般都是申請第一個進入，或停留最久的國家。

2. 收到入學許可後，務必要先檢查姓名及出生日期是否正確，這兩筆資料一定要和護照上的相同。然後再檢查報到日期是否合理，及學生顧問簽名是否遺漏，若有任何問題，則應附上正確資料後寄回學校，要求核發新的入學許可。若上述資料皆正確無誤，則應備妥其他文件後，於報到日期的九十天以內，向美國在台協會申請學生簽證。

3. 下列文件的正本有助於簽證官做出決定：

⑴ 最近的個人所得稅扣繳憑單正本。

⑵ 在職證明並註明任職期間。

⑶ 公司准假函。

⑷ 個人銀行存摺(非銀行結存表)、財力證明書。如果有工作，請攜帶名片。如果是借貸來支付學費，則必須告知畢業後還錢的方式。

⑸ 在台灣的不動產地契或其他投資證明。

⑹ 學歷證件（畢業證書與成績單）。

(7) 商業執照、駕照。

(8) 兒童申請人的學業成績單。

(9) TOEFL、TOEIC、GRE 或 GMAT 的考試成績單（簽證官一般認為，學習動機強且認真的學生，在申請美國學校的入學許可前，會參加此類考試。所以此類考試的成績單，可以證明申請人重視其留學計劃）

(10) 與美國學校來往的電子郵件，特別是和學校討論到獎學金，或其他財力援助的電子郵件

4. 開始申請前，可先瀏覽美國政府部門的網頁，或美國大使館與領事館網頁，以了解正確的申請程序。

5. 不可在向美國學校報到的 90 天前即開始申請簽證，因為簽證法規禁止簽證官在 90 天前或更早就開始處理此類申請。

6. 面試時要儘量放鬆自己，以免過度緊張影響表現。

7. 留學面談主要以英文進行。但儘量不要死記答案，這樣會降低取得簽證的機會。而且簽證官提問時，都會儘可能避免讓你使用已經準備好的演講稿，因為他們的目的，是要了解你赴美的真正意圖。

8. 根據美國移民法，領事官員必須視所有的申請人都有移民意圖，所以面談時，除了要有充分的證明文件外，更要誠實以對。切記，面談時愈誠實，獲得簽證官信任的可能性就愈高。

9. 面談時，要把精力集中在簽證官所提的問題上，不要回答自己已準備好，但簽證官根本沒問的問題。然後儘量以簡潔而直接的話來回答。

10. 萬一聽不懂或聽不清楚簽證官講的話，不要當場楞在那裡，可以說 "Excuse me. Could you please repeat slowly?"、"Pardon me."或是 "I beg your pardon."

第 2 章 英國留學簽證

英國留學簽證申請程序

事　項	內　　　　　　容
申請單位	英國貿易文化辦事處 簽證組 地址：台北市仁愛路二段 99 號福記大樓 10 樓 電話：（02）2192-7045 傳真：（02）2393-1985
收件時間	週一至週五，AM 9:00-11:00（假日除外） 請於 AM10:00 前至簽證組領取號碼牌 申請者可於申請後三～四天領取簽證，旺季則會延長
領件時間	週一至週五，PM 2:00－4:00（假日除外）
費　用	新台幣兩千兩百元整，會依匯率稍作調整
相關文件	1. 申請者事先須將申請表格 IM2A 及 IM2S 用英文正楷填寫完整，並由申請者親自簽名。其簽名必須與護照上之簽名相符 2. 六個月以上有效期之護照正本，護照上必須由持照者親自簽名 3. 半年內 2 吋相片一張，黏貼於表格 IM2A 指示處 4. 銀行開立包含學費及生活費之存款證明，此存款證明，必須是填妥表格後一個月內，由銀行所開出之證明或存摺 5. 學校所開立之入學許可證明並自備影本，這必須是全職學生課程，也就是一週至少上課 15 個小時的課程 6. 最高學歷證明並自備影本 7. 之前在英國就讀之紀錄 8. 十八歲以下之學生須附父母同意函

英國留學簽證相關注意事項

1. 簽證有效期即停留效期，在此期限內可以不限次數入境英國，但在簽證到期前須離開英國。

2. 英國簽證官對有以下情況者，可能會拒發簽證。

   ⑴ 目前在台灣的大學唸書的學生，打算退學然後出國留學。簽證官會認為其有很大的移民傾向。

   ⑵ 資金來源不明。學生家長雖然很有錢，但工作單位或公司卻沒有正式註冊，簽證官會懷疑是臨時借錢留學，其本身並無能力供子女出國留學。

   ⑶ 資料作假或說謊。

第 3 章　加拿大留學簽證

加拿大留學簽證申請程序

事　　項	內　　　　　　　　　　容
申請單位	加拿大駐台北貿易辦事處　簽證組 地址：台北市復興北路 369 號 2 樓（保富通商大樓） 電話：（02）2544-3410 傳眞：（02）2544-3594 網址：http://canada.org.tw
送件時間	AM 9:00-11:00
領件時間	PM 2:00-4:00，申請人請於次一工作日下午領件或面談
相關文件	1. 最近照片一張 2. 簽證手續費：台幣 3125 元。請以跨行電匯方式在台灣任何一家銀行繳納。恕不接受自動提款機或網路電子銀行轉帳，也無法接受匯票或支票繳款。送件後概不退費。

	3. 學生許可證申請表（含 TPS-006 及 TPS-007 兩份表格）
相	4. 學校入學許可二份(正本或影本皆可)
	5. 父母財力證明，例如：銀行存款證明
關	6. 十八歲以下之申請人，必須要有一位居住在加拿大的
	加國公民或移民當監護人，並附上經公證的監護信函，
	其內容應包括：
文	⑴ 監護人是年滿十九歲以上的成年人
	⑵ 監護人在加拿大的地址及電話
	⑶ 監護人已獲准在緊急狀況時，代替父母做決定
件	⑷ 監護人的簽名
	※ 學生許可證核發後，簽證組會以信件或電話通知您領件。

加拿大留學簽證相關注意事項

1. 除了研習短期語言課程者外，任何前往加拿大攻讀學術性、專業性或職業訓練課程者，都必須要有學生准證。

2. 若打算前往加拿大讀英文或法文，且課程少於三個月，則只需有訪客簽證即可。

3. 前往加拿大時，請攜帶學校之入學許可，以便在入關時供移民官查驗。完成課程後不可繼續就讀或轉校就讀，必須立刻離境。

4. 若打算在加拿大停留超過六個月，則必須通過體檢。簽證申請表附有體檢表及體檢指定醫師名單，至少要在開課前四星期完成體檢。

5. 填寫申請表時，若資料不全或不正確，將導致簽證被拒。

6. 重要事項
   ⑴ 護照必須至少留有一頁空白簽證頁
   ⑵ 加拿大簽證有效期不能比護照有效期長
   ⑶ 一旦核發新簽證，則原本仍有效的加拿大簽證將被註銷

7. 如要申請多次入境，則應在申請表上選擇多次，並繳交正確的費用，否則一律會被視為申請單次入境簽證。

第4章 澳洲留學簽證

澳洲留學簽證申請程序

事　　項	內　　　　　　　　　容
申請單位	澳大利亞商工辦事處 簽證服務處 地址：台北市基隆路一段 333 號 2605 室 電話：（02）8725-4250 傳眞：（02）2757-6040 網址：http://www.australia.org.tw
收件及 領件時間	週一至週五，AM 9:30－12:00 申請時間：十個工作天
費　　用	新台幣一萬零八百元整（請以現金或支票付費） 支票抬頭請填：澳大利亞商工辦事處
相 關 資 料	1. 簽證申請表 157A 並附 2 吋近照一張 2. 電子海外學生註冊確認書（Electronic Confirmation of Enrollment for overseas students） 3. 身份證，戶口名簿，或戶籍謄本（任一即可） 　（※請同時提出正本及影印本） 4. 護照正本及身體檢查報告 5. 如未滿十八歲，請提出下列其中一項證明： ⑴ 父母或監護人，將同行前往澳洲；父母或監護人已經安排你與在澳洲年滿 21 歲以上的「親戚」同住；例如：兄弟、姊妹、祖父母、叔舅、姨嬸或甥姪等，須由在澳洲的親戚提出證明關係之【宣誓聲明 Statutory Declaration】及【良民證】 ⑵ 由即將就讀的澳洲教育單位提出一份簽妥的聲明，證實其將負責在澳洲的各項生活安排，例如：住宿、支援、及一般福利措施 6. 財力證明

第 5 章　日本留學簽證

日本留學簽證申請程序

事　項	內　　　　　容
申請單位	日本交流協會 簽證室 地址：台北市慶城街 28 號 1 樓（通泰商業大樓） 電話：（02）2713-8000 網址：http://www.koryutk.org.tw/indext.htm 高雄事務所 地址：高雄市和平一路 87 號 9 樓 電話：（07）771-4008 網址：http://www.koryutk.org.tw/indext.htm
上班時間	週一至週五，AM 9:15-11:30，PM 2:00-4:00 星期五下午不受理申請，只辦理領件 星期六、日和中、日國定假日不上班 申請所需時間：一個工作天
相關文件	1. 簽證申請表格一份 2. 護照正本（三個月以上的有效期），注意，以下情況不受理申請：雙重簽名者、前簽名劃掉蓋章再簽者、前簽名擦掉再簽者 3. 身分證影本 4. 兩吋照片一張（6 個月內近照） 5. 簽證費用： 　⑴ 數次簽證：簽證費：1700 元 　　五年有效，不限使用次數，每次停留期間 90 日 　⑵ 單次簽證：簽證費：900 元 　　三個月有效，僅限使用一次，停留期間 90 日 　⑶ 過境簽證：簽證費：200 元 　　四個月內可來回目的國，途中各進入日本一次，停留期間 15 日

日本留學簽證相關注意事項

1. 簽證之有效期間：（即簽證受理後於有效期間內須入境日本，
   否則失效）
   數次：三年內有效
   單次：三個月內有效
   過境：可二次，四個月內有效

2. 如果辦理護照時間超過半年，則簽證用照片須與護照相片不同。

3. 雲林縣以南(如：嘉義、台南、高雄、屏東、台東、澎湖)均由
   高雄交流協會送件。

4. 簽證申請表的簽名欄須由本人簽名，且要與護照上的簽名相同
   (以簽寫中文姓名較佳，若簽寫英文姓名則須為草寫，絕不能以
   正楷簽名)。

5. 未成年子女的簽證申請表須由父母代簽者，除代簽當事人姓名
   外，亦須簽上代簽人姓名。

6. 申請表上的住家電話欄與公司機關電話欄，至少要填寫其中一
   項。

7. 曾經申請過日本簽證者，須附上舊日簽（若遺失，則須補報告
   書，有時亦須本人親自面談）。舊護照遺失者辦理日本簽證時，
   須附「護照遺失報案申請書」及「歷次出入境證明」，並由本
   人親自前往辦理。若持 MRP 新護照辦理單次簽證時，須附上舊
   護照，若無舊護照或舊護照遺失者，須向境管局申請五年內出
   入境資料。

第 6 章 德國留學簽證

德國留學簽證申請程序

事　　項	內　　　　　　　　容
申 請 單 位	德國在台協會　簽證組 地址：台北市民生東路 3 段 2 號 4 樓 電話：（02）2518-4088；（02）2501-6188　分機 304 傳真：（02）2501-6139
面 談 及 簽 證 業 務 時 間	週一至週五：AM 8:30-12:00 處理時間：兩個工作天
申請學生簽證	週一至週四：PM 2:00-3:30
簽證有效期	發照日起半年
費　　用	有效期為一個月者 NT$640 有效期為三個月者 NT$1220 有效期為一年者 NT$1740
相　　關　　文　　件	1. 護照正本（持照者親自簽名，效期至少三個月以上） 2. 申請表一份(申請者親自簽名) 3. 行程表一份 4. 二吋近照一張 5. 身份證影本一份 6. 外籍人士附外僑居留證影本一份 7. 在領取簽證時，須出示歐洲來回且機位確定之有效機票 8. 十八歲以下孩童須個別申辦簽證，且申請表格須父母雙方或法定代理人簽字，並附上父母同意書及父母身份證影本

第 **7** 章　紐西蘭留學簽證

紐西蘭留學簽證申請程序

事　項	內　　　　　　容
申請單位	紐西蘭商工辦事處 地址：台北市信義區基隆路 1 段 333 號國貿大樓 25 樓 2501 室 電話：（02）2757-7060 傳眞：（02）2757-6974
簽證受理	週一至週五，AM 9:00-12:00
簽證領取	週一至週五，PM 2:00-4:30
處理時間	兩個工作天
費　用	新台幣三千七百五十元
相 關 文 件	1. 塡妥學生簽證申請表格，並由本人簽名 2. 護照有效期須比停留期間多三個月 3. 三個月內兩吋近照一張 4. 學校入學許可正本（Offer of Place），須包括課程名稱、就讀時間及應繳學費 5. 學費收據正本；或匯款至學校帳戶的證明，但所匯之金額及帳戶名稱須與入學許可或通知繳費信函上相符 6. 由學校或提供住宿之家庭所出具的住宿擔保書正本 7. 一年課程須有財力證明紐幣 7000 元以上；短於三十六週的課程每月須有紐幣 1000 元以上（財力證明可爲申請人，或財力擔保人名下之銀行存款證明） 8. 非申請人名下之存款證明，須另附一份財力擔保書，並由財力擔保人簽名 9. 已於或將於紐西蘭就讀兩年以上長期課程者，須提供體檢報告 10.十七歲以上且將於紐西蘭就讀兩年以上長期課程者，須提供良民證 11.戶籍謄本或戶口名簿影本 12.若已在紐西蘭就讀，而回台灣提出延長學生簽證者，須出示前一學年的成績單及出席率證明

紐西蘭留學簽證相關注意事項

1. 取得紐西蘭技術學院，或大學三年以上畢業證書者，可於申請紐西蘭一般技術類別移民時，額外獲得二分，並免除兩年以上工作經驗之要求。

2. 在紐西蘭技術學院或大學，攻讀三年以上之學位者，可於就學期間兼職。每週兼職時間不得超過十五小時。

3. 醫療保險雖非強制性，但所有海外學生就醫都必須負擔高額醫療費用，因此特別建議於赴紐西蘭就讀前，預先規劃保險計畫。

4. 如就讀三個月以下單項課程者，可申請觀光簽證，但必須於表格內註明求學意願。

5. 學期內常曠課者，移民局有權取消其學生簽證。

6. 新舊護照不可同時使用，請至本組或紐西蘭各地移民局轉移有效簽證至新護照內。

7. 如學校出具之文件正本無法即時取得，簽證組亦接受由學校傳真至本組之文件。

1. *Computer Science*

> Mr. Lin graduated from Tsing Hua University, College of Electrical Engineering and Computer Science three years ago. He has decided to study abroad in the USA at the end of the year. Now he is preparing for that.

(*C* : *Consular official* *L* : *Mr. Lin*)

C : What is your purpose in applying for a visa?

L : My purpose is to study computer science at Columbia University.

C : Why do you choose computer science as a major?

L : My father taught electrical engineering in a university, and so I naturally got interested in it. He always encouraged me to be interested in machines. And I think there is going to be more and more activity in this field in Taiwan.

C : How will you pay all your expenses during your stay in the States?

L : My uncle, who runs a supermarket in New York, has guaranteed my complete support. And my father will also help to pay my living expenses in the U.S.

①. 資訊工程

> 林先生三年前從清大電機工程系畢業。他打算在年底
> 前往美國留學。他現在正在為留學的相關事宜做準備。

（ *C* ：簽證官　 *L* ：林先生）

簽證官： 你申請簽證的目的是什麼？

林先生： 我的目的是到哥倫比亞大學唸資訊工程。

簽證官： 你為什麼要選資訊工程當主修？

林先生： 我父親在大學教電機工程，所以我自然會對電子工程感
興趣。我父親一直鼓勵我對機械產生興趣，而且我認為
這個行業在台灣會越來越興盛。

簽證官： 你怎麼支付你留美期間所有的費用？

林先生： 我叔叔在紐約經營超級市場，他答應完全支持我。而且
我父親也會資助我在美國的生活費。

C : What will you do after finishing your studies in the States?

L : I expect to return to the company where I am working now. I'll probably be working as the manager of a department that deals with computers.

C : How long will you stay in the States?

L : I want to get a master's degree, so I plan to be there for about two years.

簽證官： 你在美國唸完書後要做什麼？

林先生： 我希望能回到我目前工作的公司，我可能會擔任電腦部
門的經理。

簽證官： 你將在美國停留多久？

林先生： 我想拿到碩士學位，所以我打算在那裡待兩年左右。

2. Business Administration

> Mr. Lee is 28 years old. Now he is a sales manager at PACE Trading Company. In order to realize his ambitions in business, he has decided to go abroad and get a master's degree in business administration.

(*C* : *Consular official* *L* : *Mr. Lee*)

C : Please sit down. What is your name?

L : My name is Chung-hsin Lee.

C : What are you doing now?

L : I'm working for a foreign trading company in the export department.

C : Why did you choose business administration as a major?

L : Because we have to improve our methods of business organization and management and find new ways to successfully invest our income in international business. We now need well-trained people to help diversify our economy.

②. 企 管

> 李先生今年二十八歲。他目前是 PACE 貿易公司的業務經理。爲了要在商業方面實現自己的抱負,他決定要出國,並拿一個企管碩士學位回來。

（ *C*：簽證官 　*L*：李先生 ）

簽證官：　請坐。請問你叫什麼名字?

李先生：　我叫李忠信。

簽證官：　你目前從事什麼工作?

李先生：　我在一家外貿公司的出口部工作。

簽證官：　你爲什麼選企管作爲主修?

李先生：　因爲我們必須改善企業組織與經營的方法,並尋找新的途徑,好將我們的收入成功地投資在國際企業中。我們現在需要的是訓練有素的人,才能讓我們的經濟變得多元化。

C : Why do you want to go to America?

L : Because I want to study my major, business Administration, there. And when it comes to business administration, the management concepts of American corporations are worth learning. So I need to go to America and continue to study in my major subject.

C : After graduation, will you find a job in America?

L : Certainly not. I want to go back to Taiwan, because I have to do something for my country.

C : What will you do when you come home?

L : I want to engage in foreign trade and establish my own trading company. I wish to be a successful businessman.

C : Do you feel your English is good enough to complete an MBA course?

L : Yes. I received a high score on the TOEFL and GMAT. And I am supposed to take an ESL language course to improve my English ability further.

C : Who will take financial responsibility for you during your stay in the States?

L : My father will take financial responsibility for me during my stay in the States.

簽證官： 你為什麼想去美國？

李先生： 因為我想去那裡研讀我的主修科目——企業管理。而一談到企業管理，美國公司的經營理念很值得學習。所以我需要到美國去，並繼續攻讀我的主修科目。

簽證官： 畢業之後，你會在美國找工作嗎？

李先生： 絕對不會。我要回台灣，因為我必須為我的國家盡點力。

簽證官： 你回國後要做什麼？

李先生： 我想從事外貿，並創立自己的貿易公司。我希望成為一個成功的企業家。

簽證官： 你覺得你的英文有好到足以完成企管碩士的課程嗎？

李先生： 可以，我的托福和 GMAT 都得高分，而且我應該會唸 ESL 語言課程，使我的英文更進步。

簽證官： 在你留美期間，誰要負擔你的經濟？

李先生： 我父親在我留美期間，會負擔我的經濟。

C : What does your father do?

L : He is a plant manager at Formosa Plastics
Corporation. He told me that he will pay my tuition
and living expenses.

C : How long do you expect to be there?

L : I will be there for three years.

C : Good. You may go now.

L : Thank you, sir.

簽證官： 你父親從事什麼行業？

李先生： 他是台塑公司的廠長。他跟我說，他會支付我的學費和
生活費。

簽證官： 你想在那裡待多久？

李先生： 我將在那裡待三年。

簽證官： 好，你現在可以走了。

李先生： 謝謝你，先生。

③. *Genetic Engineering*

> Mr. Huang is ready to graduate from Chung Hsing University this June. In order to pursue his career goal, he plans to apply for an American visa, and go to study further at Virginia University.

(***C*** : *Consular official* ***H*** : *Mr. Huang*)

C : What is your major?

H : I'm majoring in biochemistry.

C : Do you have any particular reason to study in America?

H : Yes. I hope to study genetic engineering but there are no good programs in this field here. And America is the most advanced country in this field.

C : Why do you want to study it?

H : Because it relates intimately to my major, biochemistry science, and I think it will be an area of future technological development. I want to be a pioneer in this field here in Taiwan.

③ 遺傳工程學

> 黃先生今年六月將從中興大學畢業。爲了追求他的生涯目標，他打算要申請美國簽證，然後到維吉尼亞大學進修。

（ *C*：簽證官　*H*：黃先生）

簽證官： 你主修什麼？

黃先生： 我主修生物化學。

簽證官： 你到美國唸書有什麼特別的原因嗎？

黃先生： 有。我想唸遺傳工程，但是就這個領域來說，這裡並沒有好的課程。而且美國在這方面是最先進的。

簽證官： 你爲什麼想唸這門學科？

黃先生： 因爲它和我主修的生物化學密切相關，而且我認爲它將是未來科技發展的領域。我想成爲台灣在這個領域的先驅。

C : Who is your sponsor?

H : Well, I've got a full scholarship from Virginia University. Besides, my uncle has promised to pay my living expenses.

C : What is he doing for a living?

H : He is a doctor practicing obstetrics in Tainan.

C : What do you plan to do when you earn your degree?

H : I'll return to Taiwan, and I intend to engage in genetic engineering. Maybe I'll teach in college while I engage in my studies.

C : That's all. You may leave now.

H : Thank you, sir.

簽證官： 誰是你的贊助人？

黃先生： 嗯，我已經拿到維吉尼亞大學的全額獎學金。而且，我叔叔也答應要資助我的生活費。

簽證官： 他以什麼維生？

黃先生： 他在台南當婦產科醫生。

簽證官： 你拿到學位以後，打算做什麼？

黃先生： 我將回到台灣，然後我打算全心投入於遺傳工程中。也許我會一邊在大學授課，一邊從事我的研究。

簽證官： 就這樣，你現在可以走了。

黃先生： 謝謝你，先生。

4. *Education*

Miss Yang plans to study abroad, so she has to get an American visa. She has already prepared all the necessary documents. Now she is sitting in front of the Consular official.

(*I* : *Consular official* *Y* : *Miss Yang*)

Y : Morning, sir.

I : Morning. How are you?

Y : Fine, just a little bit nervous. (*smile*)

I : Would you mind answering a few questions?

Y : Certainly not. Please go ahead.

I : Why will you go to the U.S.?

Y : Because I want to get an M.A. and a Ph.D. there.

I : What is your major?

Y : I majored in education.

I : What are you doing now?

Y : I'm a graduate student at Taiwan University.

4. 教 育

楊小姐打算出國留學，所以她必須拿到美國簽證。她已經準備好所有必備的文件了。現在楊小姐正坐在簽證官面前。

（ *I*：簽證官　　*Y*：楊小姐 ）

楊小姐：早安，先生。

簽證官：早安。妳好嗎？

楊小姐：還好，只是有一點緊張。（微笑）

簽證官：妳不介意回答幾個問題吧？

楊小姐：當然不介意，請問。

簽證官：妳為什麼要去美國？

楊小姐：因為我想去那裡拿一個碩士學位和一個博士學位。

簽證官：妳主修什麼？

楊小姐：我主修教育。

簽證官：妳目前從事什麼行業？

楊小姐：我是台大的研究生。

I : Why did you happen to choose Indiana State University?

Y : My professor recommended the university. And the best courses in education are offered at Indiana State University.

I : How about the funding?

Y : My father will pay all my expenses.

I : Where will your father get the funds from?

Y : He plans to use his savings and regular salary. He earns about NT$ 1,200,000 per year.

I : Do you think your English is good enough to understand lectures in graduate school?

Y : Yes, I have wanted to study abroad for a long time, so I have studied English very hard. And I minored in English literature in university.

I : Give me your admission letter.

Y : OK, here you are.

I : Your transcripts?

Y : May I open it for you?

I : OK. (*Takes a quick look.*)

簽證官： 妳爲什麼會選印地安那州立大學？

楊小姐： 我的教授推薦的，而且印地安那州立大學提供最優秀的
教育課程。

簽證官： 妳的資金從哪裡來？

楊小姐： 我父親會資助我全部的費用。

簽證官： 妳的父親從哪裡得到這筆資金？

楊小姐： 他打算用他的存款和薪水。他一年大約賺新台幣一百二
十萬元。

簽證官： 妳認爲妳的英文可以聽得懂研究所的課嗎？

楊小姐： 可以，我很久以前就想要出國留學了，所以我很努力
學英文，並且在大學輔修英國文學。

簽證官： 請把妳的入學許可給我。

楊小姐： 好的，在這裡。

簽證官： 妳的成績單呢？

楊小姐： 要我打開給你看嗎？

簽證官： 好的。（很快地看了一下。）

I : I see. How long do you plan to stay in the U.S.?

Y : I expect it to take five years for me to earn my M.A. and Ph.D. I hope it doesn't take any longer.

I : Do you have any plans after your study in the United States?

Y : I've wanted to be a professor ever since I was little. I'll come back to my country and be a teacher in my old school. I hope to have a chance to apply what I learn.

I : Fine. That's all. You may leave now.

Y : Thank you. Good-bye.

簽證官： 我知道了。妳打算在美國停留多久？

楊小姐： 我想花五年的時間拿到碩士和博士學位，我希望不會花更久的時間。

簽證官： 妳在美國唸完書後，有任何計劃嗎？

楊小姐： 我從小就想當教授，我會回到我的國家，並在我的母校當老師。我希望能有學以致用的機會。

簽證官： 很好。就這樣。妳現在可以走了。

楊小姐： 謝謝你，再見。

(5.) *International Relations*

Mr. Wang comes from Taitung. He has been taking English classes since he graduated from college three years ago. His personal goal is to study international relations in the U.S. as soon as he has earned enough money.

(**C** : *Consular official* **W** : *Mr. Wang*)

C : Your name and present address, please?

W : My name is Wang Chung-ming. I live in Taipei at Tong Hua Street, Lane200, Number 11, 4th Floor.

C : What's your major?

W : My major field of study is political science. I graduated from Chengchi University three years ago.

C : What have you been doing since college?

W : I work for a publishing company as a staff member of the editing section.

C : Now, you want to study in America. Is there any special reason?

W : Yes. I take a special interest in international relations, the study of which is mostly concentrated in America. Mr. Robison, who is one of my academic role models, has promised to be my advisor.

5. 國際關係

> 　　王先生來自台東。三年前從大學畢業後,他一直都有在上英文課。他的個人目標是等他一存夠錢之後,就馬上到美國去唸國際關係。

(*C* : 簽證官　*W* : 王先生)

簽證官：請問你的名字和現在的住址?

王先生：我叫王忠明,住在台北市通化街 200 巷 11 號 4 樓。

簽證官：你主修什麼?

王先生：我主要的研究領域是政治學,三年前畢業於政大。

簽證官：大學畢業後,你一直在做什麼?

王先生：我在一家出版公司擔任編輯部門的成員之一。

簽證官：現在你要到美國去唸書,有什麼特別原因嗎?

王先生：有的,我對國際關係特別感興趣,而這些研究大部分集中在美國。羅賓遜先生,他是我在學術方面的偶像之一,答應要當我的指導教授。

C : How long do you plan to stay there?

W : As soon as I receive a doctoral degree, I will return to Taiwan and teach at my alma mater.

C : Who will pay for all the expenses during your stay in America?

W : I've got a research assistantship from American University and I've saved up for study abroad, so I can meet the other expenses.

C : Won't you have problems understanding lectures in English?

W : No. I've worked hard enough to improve my English, so I think I'll do well.

C : Have you ever applied for a visa before?

W : No, never.

C : Any relatives in the U.S.?

W : No.

C : That's enough. You may leave now.

W : Thanks a lot.

簽證官： 你打算在那裡待多久？

王先生： 我一拿到博士學位，就會回台灣，到我的母校教書。

簽證官： 在你留美期間，誰會支付你所有的費用？

王先生： 我已經得到美國大學的研究助理獎金，而且也有存錢準備留學，所以可以支付其他的費用。

簽證官： 你要聽懂英文授課，有沒有任何問題？

王先生： 沒有，我已經很努力在提昇我的英文程度了，所以我想我可以表現得很好。

簽證官： 你以前曾經申請過簽證嗎？

王先生： 沒有，從來沒有。

簽證官： 在美國有任何親戚嗎？

王先生： 沒有。

簽證官： 這樣就夠了，你現在可以走了。

王先生： 多謝。

6. *Economics*

Miss Wu will graduate this June. She wants to study abroad and get advanced knowledge and more professional training to support her career goal — working as an analyst in the Taiwan Economic Development & Research Academy.

(*C* : *Interviewer* *W* : *Miss Wu*)

C : Miss Wu, I understand you're a grad student at National Sun Yat-sen University. What is your major?

W : I major in economics.

C : What specific field of economics are you interested in?

W : I'm interested in socioeconomics.

C : What are you planning to do for your thesis?

W : Well, my topic will be "Economic Development and the Crime Rate." I have decided to analyze the relationship between the increase in criminal cases and the economic recession.

C : I see. You applied at California State University in Los Angeles. Why did you choose this university?

W : It provides the best program. I think it'll be very helpful in supporting of my research.

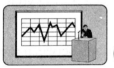

6. 經 濟

> 吳小姐將在今年六月畢業。她想到國外唸書，以獲得更高深的知識和更專業的訓練，好幫助她達成事業上的目標——在「台灣經濟發展研究院」擔任分析人員。

（ *C*：簽證官　*W*：吳小姐）

簽證官： 吳小姐，我知道妳是國立中山大學的研究生。妳主修什麼？

吳小姐： 我主修經濟學。

簽證官： 妳對經濟學的哪個領域特別感興趣？

吳小姐： 我對社會經濟學有興趣。

簽證官： 妳的畢業論文打算做什麼？

吳小姐： 嗯，我將以「經濟發展和犯罪率」為題。我已經決定要分析刑事案件的增加與經濟衰退的關係。

簽證官： 我了解了。妳申請的是洛杉磯的加州大學。為什麼要選這所大學？

吳小姐： 因為這所大學提供最棒的課程。我認為那對我的研究會很有幫助。

C : What would be your subject of research during your stay in the United States?

W : I would like to study economic relations between the United States and Taiwan.

C : Who is going to assure your financial support during your stay in the United States?

W : I have received a Catholic scholarship from my university.

C : Will your husband go to the U.S.A. with you?

W : No. But he will go to the U.S.A. to see me during his vacation.

C : That's all. You may leave now.

W : Thank you, sir. Good-bye.

簽證官： 妳留美期間，將以什麼做爲研究主題？

吳小姐： 我想研究美國和台灣的經濟關係。

簽證官： 在妳留美期間，誰保證會給妳經濟上的支持？

吳小姐： 我從我的大學得到天主教獎學金。

簽證官： 妳丈夫會跟妳一起去美國嗎？

吳小姐： 不。但他會在放假期間去美國探望我。

簽證官： 就這樣，妳現在可以走了。

吳小姐： 謝謝你，先生。再見。

第⑤篇 ▶ 移民簽證實況會話

Interview for Emigration

移民簽證面談訣竅

1. 面談前的準備

(1) 面談前，須準備好體檢和無犯罪紀錄證明，以及各項必備文件的正本和翻譯本。若爲技術移民，則最好將個人學經歷、輝煌紀錄、作品集整理妥當，一起帶去面談。

(2) How are you today? I am fine, thank you. And you? 這幾句話請努力熟記。因爲不管是在和移民官面談時，或是將來到了國外，都會經常用到，這是基本的問候禮節。回答時以簡單扼要爲主，對方只是問好而已，不需要回答得太冗長或太詳細。

(3) 基本上移民官都很友善，但還是會帶有個人喜好。面談時服裝宜整齊得體，不可奇裝異服，禮貌周到、面帶微笑與互相尊重是必備的，只要條件符合移民資格，移民官並不會刻意（也不允許）刁難。

2. 面談注意事項

(1) 接到面談通知信後，應看清楚面談的時間和地點，並在確認時間後，準時抵達。

(2) 面談時，移民官最想知道三件事：第一，資料是否有假；第二，當事人是否眞的想移民，並與該國一起奮鬥；最後，再評估您是否能適應該國情況，且有獨立生活的能力，而不會造成該國的負擔（因爲國外的社會福利制度較健全，國家會給予失業者極度完善的照顧與補助，但如此一來，將耗損該國大量的社會資源）。

(3) 面談結束前，移民官會告訴您通過與否及理由，要仔細聆聽，
並詢問何時可拿到 PR (移民紙)。

3. 面談時的七大禁忌

⑴ **不談負面感受**

【例】 台灣空氣很糟，治安不好。(誤)
移民是想追求更理想的生活方式。(正)

⑵ **不談隱藏的計劃**

【例】 如果我找不到工作，就只好想辦法做生意。(誤)
我一定會找到工作。或：我已經找到工作了。(正)

⑶ **不談家庭問題**

【例】 我先生當空中飛人，而我留在美國帶小孩。(誤)
我們全家會一起到當地居留。(正)

⑷ **不要談你的過錯及失敗經驗**

【例】 我前次申請沒過關，是因為英文不好。(誤)
我的語文足以應付生活所需。(正)

⑸ **不要問你應該知道的資訊**

【例】 加拿大冷不冷？

⑹ **不要問福利問題**

【例】 依我的狀況，可以得到多少社會福利？(誤)
我可以負擔自己的生活開支，不需仰賴貴國的資助。(正)

⑺ **不要猶豫得到居留權後，何時可以啟程**

【例】 我應該會在三年後，拿到退休金再過去。(誤)

4. 面談中最常見的錯誤與因應對策

面談中，如何回答移民官所提出的問題，是其核心所在，移民官審核的標準也取決於此。以下為申請者最常犯的兩種錯誤：

⑴ 被動式回答

這是最常見，也是最糟糕的一種回答。最典型的例子為：

移民官問	你在哪家公司服務？
回　　答	我在×××公司工作。(沉默)

這種回答錯在忽視移民面談的主要目的：了解你的背景和經歷。所以當問及你的公司或相關背景時，必須充分且詳細地回答，使移民官有具體的了解。較為適當的回答為：

移民官問	你在哪家公司服務？
回　　答	我在××會計師事務所擔任審計員的工作。事務所位於新竹市，總共約有一百六十名員工，××事務所是台灣四大會計師事務所之一，且為電腦化程度最高的會計師事務所。

上述回答的優點是：具體而詳細。使移民官對你的公司以及你所擔任的職位，有清晰而具體的了解，而不只是一個空洞的名字。

如果你的公司和國外知名公司有任何業務上的往來，無論是什麼關係，包括合作、代理、合資、合夥、轉投資等等，都可以一併告知移民官。當工作單位與移民國有合作關係時，將是一項非常有利的優勢，必須強調出來。

移民官問	告訴我一些關於你們公司的事。
回　　答	×××公司，是台灣大學——相當於美國的哈佛，和日本松下電機的合資公司，專門生產電器產品，去年一年的產量約為…，在台灣電器市場的佔有率約為…，我主要是從事廣告與包裝的部分，也就是行銷部門的工作。

　　這個回答把移民官最想知道的都說得清清楚楚。而且，哈佛和松下電機是移民官非常熟悉的名詞，所以當你和這兩個詞彙產生關聯之後，此刻坐在移民官前接受面試的你，就不再只是一個沒沒無聞的「申請人」，而是一個移民官能夠認同的「自己人」。儘量把自己的經歷、公司、學校、作品、牽涉到的技術、使用的設備等等，和國外（特別是申請移民國）產生連結。如果實在沒有辦法產生連結，那也應該避免說謊或捏造，可以用具體數字、事實及誠懇的態度來獲得移民官的認同。

　　總之，移民面試的目的就是要多了解你，所以不要惜言如金，請多說一點吧！也許你會擔心，萬一說太多，移民官會不會煩呢？不會的，你必須和移民官建立互動與交流。假如移民官喜歡你說，你就多說一點，若他不喜歡聽，你可以就此打住，仔細的察言觀色，以平常心對待，就像我們平常與人交往一樣。

⑵ **自我否定式**

　　謙虛是中國人的美德，但若在移民官面前誤用這種美德，則可能會使移民官產生不好的印象，甚至導致移民申請失敗。典型的例子為：

移 民 官 問	回　　答
你服務的公司是家什麼樣的公司？	別提了，只是一間又小又破的公司，才二十個人。
你是哪一所大學畢業的？	別提了，只是一間沒沒無名的私立學校而已。
你的英語程度聽起來很普通，為什麼表格上卻寫著流利呢？	我的英語確實很差，真的很抱歉，不過我會想辦法提升的…。

　　這種回答錯在自我否定。如果你服務的公司只是一間又小又破的公司，那麼在這家公司工作的你，想必更糟；如果你的學校不值得一提，那麼從這所學校畢業的你，一定也不值得一提。如此一來，移民官還有什麼理由要通過你的申請呢？較適當的回答和姿態應該是：對於自己曾經從事的一切都充滿自信與熱情，不管提到什麼，都應該以積極向上的態度和充分的信心來回答。但請切記，絕對不可淪為炫耀或捏造，否則可能會導致反效果。

移 民 官 問	回　　答
貴公司是一家什麼樣的公司？	×××公司是一家高科技公司，專攻多媒體製作，雖然規模不大，只有二、三十人，但其主要產品「×××」遊戲卻十分流行，去年在全國排行榜上名列第六…。
談談你的大學。	我畢業於交通大學，交大是台灣大學中前景十分看好的理工學院，專門為台灣的高科技產業培訓專業人才。 我主修電子工程，尤其是側重於奈米科技的研發…。
你的英語程度聽起來很普通…。	就像我取得其他的成就一樣，我的英語將會大幅進步，如果你願意給我簽證的話！

　　申請移民的過程，就等於是向該國證明自己的過程。在這場面談中，你所做的一切，無非就是想證明，你符合該國的移民資格，這場面試將是你證明自己優秀資格的最後機會。你必須爲自己所做的、所經歷的一切感到自豪，包括爲你即將在移民國獲得的成就感到自信驕傲，這才是積極的人生觀，也是確保你成功取得簽證的唯一態度。

5. 面談問題一覽表

英　文　題　目	翻　　　譯
Why do you want to go to the U.S.?	你爲什麼想去美國？
What particular things do you like in the U.S.?	你特別喜愛美國的哪一方面？
What do you think of the American economy?	你覺得美國的經濟如何？
Why would you like to settle in Los Angeles?	你爲什麼想定居在洛杉磯？
What do you know about America?	你對美國有什麼認識？
Tell me any other cities you know in America.	試舉任何你所知道的美國其他城市。
What do you think of the experience you have had in Taiwan?	你對於在台灣的生活經驗有何看法？
Do you want to go to the U.S. because you are not successful in Taiwan?	你是因爲在台灣失敗，所以才想去美國的嗎？
Why don't you go to Canada?	你爲什麼不去加拿大？
What do you know about California, the place you're going to live?	你對你將要定居的地方—加州，知道些什麼？
Tell me anything you know about San Francisco.	請告訴我你對舊金山的所有認知。

英　文　題　目	翻　　　譯
You know Canada has one of the best social welfare systems/health systems in the world. What do you think of it?	你知道加拿大是擁有世界上最健全的社會福利/醫療制度的國家之一。對此你有何看法？
Does your spouse have any plan to accompany you to America?	你的妻子打算和你一起到美國去嗎？
Have you heard anything about America in the Chinese media recently?	你最近在台灣的媒體上，有聽到任何關於美國的消息嗎？
What's your impression of California?	你對加州的印象爲何？
What do you think about the American political system?	你對美國的政治制度有何看法？
Have you been to America?	你去過美國嗎？
What is the biggest city in Canada?	加拿大最大的城市是哪一個？
Who is the president of the U.S.?	美國總統是誰？
Where are you going to settle (or live) in America?	你打算定居在美國的哪裡？
How many people are there in your family?	你們家一共有多少人？
Why are you leaving your spouse/child/parents behind?	你爲什麼要離開你的配偶/小孩/父母？
Do your parents agree with your emigration?	你的父母同意你移民嗎？
Why do you want to leave Taiwan?	你爲什麼要離開台灣？
Why don't you bring your child with you to Canada?	你爲什麼不帶小孩一起去加拿大？
Can you speak any other languages?	你會說其他任何語言嗎？
What university did you graduate from?	你是什麼大學畢業的？
Is your university famous?	你唸的那所大學有名嗎？

英　文　題　目	翻　　　譯
Tell me something about your university.	告訴我一些關於那所大學的事。
How often do you use English?	你多久使用一次英語？
Since you graduated from university more than 10 years ago, how can you keep up in the fast-changing world?	你大學畢業已經超過十年以上了，你如何在這個快速變遷的世界趕上別人呢？
What have you learnt in your university?	你在大學裡學些什麼？
Have the courses you studied in the university helped you?	你在大學唸的課程對你有幫助嗎？
Did you get any awards in the university?	你在大學時得過任何獎項嗎？
How long have you studied English?	你學英文多久了？
What kind of qualification did you get?	你擁有哪些資格證照？
Do you have any other languages or skills, which might assist you in finding a job in Canada?	你會其他任何語言或技能，能幫助你在加拿大找到工作嗎？
Do you have to speak or write English in your working environment?	你必須在你的工作環境中說寫英文嗎？
How did the training help you in your present career?	職訓對你目前的工作有什麼幫助？
What's your major?	你主修什麼？
How many employees are there in your company?	你們公司裡有多少員工？
Have you received any on-site job training?	你有受過任何現場工作訓練嗎？
You studied physics (or other field), so why do you want to be a computer programmer?	你唸的是物理學（或其他領域），為什麼要當電腦程式設計員呢？

英　文　題　目	翻　　　譯
Do you have any professional licenses/certificates?	你有任何專業的執照或證照嗎？
Can you use a computer?	你會操作電腦嗎？
In what company are you working at present?	你目前在哪一家公司工作？
Can you tell me something about your company?	可以告訴我一些關於你公司的事嗎？
Have you received any professional training?	你受過任何專業訓練嗎？
Tell me about one of your biggest achievements.	告訴我你最大的成就之一。
How long have you been working in the company?	你在這家公司工作多久了？
Have you been working in this firm since your graduation?	你從畢業之後，就待在這家公司嗎？
How long have you been in the position?	你擔任這個職位多久了？
What is your position in your company?	你在公司裡擔任什麼職位？
How many people do you supervise?	你手下有幾位員工？
What's the main business of your company?	貴公司的主要業務是什麼？
What have you done in your work?	你在工作上有何貢獻？
What are your responsibilities?	你負責什麼工作？
What's your routine work?	你的例行工作是什麼？
Tell me your colleagues' job titles.	請描述你同事的職稱。
Why did you work in the same company for so long?	你為什麼在同一家公司工作這麼久？
Do you know any company in America which offers the same service as your company?	你知道任何一家和貴公司業務性質相同的美國公司嗎？

英　文　題　目	翻　　譯
What are your achievements?	你有哪些成就？
Do you have a reference letter from your present employer?	你有現任雇主的推薦函嗎？
After you land in America, what sort of job you plan to look for and how long do you believe it will take you before you can successfully get a job offer?	在你定居美國之後，你打算找哪一種工作？你認為要花多久的時間才能成功找到一份工作？
How can you find a job in Australia?	你如何在澳洲找到一份工作？
Why do you think you can live and be successful in Canada at your age?	依你的年紀，你為什麼覺得自己可以成功地定居在加拿大呢？
Why do you think you can be successful in America, while many other immigrants have failed in their career?	當看過這麼多在美國事業失敗的移民例子後，為什麼你還覺得自己會成功呢？
If I approve your application, do you think you will have any problems adapting to the new life style in Australia? If no, tell me why you have confidence that you can adapt to the new environment. What plans have you made for living in Australia?	假如我核准你的申請，你覺得自己在適應澳洲的全新生活方式時，會不會有任何困難？假如沒有，告訴我為什麼你有把握可以適應新環境。你擬定了什麼計劃嗎？
Do you have any idea about the job market in your occupation in Canada?	在加拿大的就業市場中，你對自己所從事的行業有任何了解嗎？
What are you going to do if you cannot find a job in Australia? How will your friends help you?	假如你在澳洲找不到工作的話，你打算怎麼辦？你的朋友會怎麼幫你？
What is the first important thing you are going to do after your arrival in Canada?	當你抵達加拿大之後，你覺得最重要且會第一個去做的事情是什麼？

英　　文　　題　　目	翻　　　　譯
What are your relatives (friends) doing in America?	你的親戚（朋友）在美國從事什麼行業？
You know a lot of Taiwanese have come back from Canada. What do you think about it?	你知道有很多台灣人從加拿大回來，對此你有什麼看法？
Can you tell me something about your career?	可以告訴我一些關於你工作上的事嗎？
Why are you certain that you can be a successful immigrant?	你為什麼確信自己能夠當個成功的移民者？
How can you survive in Canada?	你如何在加拿大生存？
Have you done any research into job opportunities in America?	你曾經對美國的就業機會做過任何研究嗎？
Do you have enough money to support yourself and your family if you can't find a job immediately?	如果你無法馬上找到工作，你有足夠的錢負擔自己和家人的生活開銷嗎？
Do you have any relatives or friends in Australia who could assist you?	你在澳洲有任何可以幫助你的親戚或朋友嗎？
What's your career objective?	你的工作目標是什麼？
How much do you have in transferable funds and other personal assets? Do you have a summary of your assets?	你擁有多少流動資金和個人不動產？你有資產清單嗎？
Do you know anything about the present employment situation in Canada?	你了解加拿大目前的就業情況嗎？
What are you going to do if you have no money and nobody is willing to help you?	假如你沒錢，而且又沒有人可以幫你，你會怎麼辦？

Interview for Emigration 1

> Two years ago, Miss Lee's family decided to emigrate to the U.S. But at that time, Miss Lee was a sophomore in Chiao Tung University. In order to complete her college education, Miss Lee thought that she needed to stay Taiwan for two more years. Now she is ready to graduate, so she is applying for a visa.

(*C* : *Consular official* *L* : *Miss Lee*)

C : Have a seat, please. May I have your name and birthdate?

L : My name is Lee Shu-hui and I was born on October first, 1981.

C : How many are there in your family?

L : We're four in all. But my parents and brother have already gone to the U.S.

C : Do your parents have U.S. citizenship?

L : Yes, they do. They sent me a letter of invitation.

C : You are single, aren't you?

L : Yes. I have no idea of getting married in the near future.

移民面談 1

> 　　兩年前，李小姐的家人決定移民到美國。但當時李小姐還是交大二年級的學生。為了完成大學學業，李小姐心想，她必須在台灣多待兩年。現在李小姐即將畢業了，所以她準備要申請簽證。

（**C**：簽證官　**L**：李小姐）

簽證官：請坐。請問妳的名字和生日？

李小姐：我叫李淑慧，1981 年 10 月 1 日生。

簽證官：妳家裡有幾個人？

李小姐：我家共有四個人，但是我的父母和哥哥已經到美國去了。

簽證官：妳父母有美國公民權嗎？

李小姐：是的，他們有，他們寫信來要我去。

簽證官：妳目前單身，對不對？

李小姐：是的，我近期內還不打算結婚。

C : What are you going to do in the U.S.?

L : For the first year, I'm going to help my parents in their supermarket during the daytime and go to a language training school at night. After that I'll go to graduate school to continue my study.

C : Fine. That's all. Good luck to you.

L : Thank you. Good-bye.

簽證官： 妳在美國要做什麼？

李小姐： 第一年，我白天會到我父母開的超級市場幫忙，晚上到
語言訓練班上課。之後會上研究所繼續唸書。

簽證官： 好，就這樣，祝妳好運。

李小姐： 謝謝你，再見。

Interview for Emigration 2

Mr. Lu has worked in the Runner shoe company for five years. His best friend, Mr. Wu, established a shoe factory in the U.S. two years ago. He called Mr. Lu and invited him to work at his factory. He said that he really needed a creative shoe designer.

(*C* : *Consular official* *L* : *Mr. Lu*)

C : What is your motive for emigrating to America?

L : My friend, who has lived for years in America asked me to go to America and work with him.

C : Who did you get the letter of invitation from?

L : I got it from my friend Mr. Wu, who is in charge of a shoe factory in New York.

C : What's your job in Taiwan?

L : I'm a shoe designer. I've worked for the Runner shoe company for five years.

C : Do you have a job offer in America?

L : Yes, I have. My friend told me that I could work as a creative director in his factory.

移民面談 2

盧先生在 Runner 鞋公司已經工作五年了。而他最要好的朋友，吳先生，兩年前在美國開了一家鞋工廠。他打電話給盧先生，並邀請他成為工廠的一員。他說他真的很需要一位有創意的鞋子設計師。

（*C*：簽證官　*L*：盧先生）

簽證官：　你移民美國的動機是什麼？

盧先生：　我的朋友在美國待了幾年，要我到美國去和他一起工作。

簽證官：　你從誰那裡得到邀請函？

盧先生：　我從我的朋友吳先生那裡得到的，他在紐約負責一家鞋工廠。

簽證官：　你在台灣從事什麼行業？

盧先生：　我是個鞋子設計師。我在 Runner 鞋公司工作了五年。

簽證官：　你在美國有工作機會嗎？

盧先生：　是的，我有。我朋友說，我可以在他的工廠擔任創意總監一職。

C : How much money will you earn in a week?

L : I'm supposed to be paid 500 dollars a week.

C : What is your final destination in the United States?

L : It will be New York.

C : Dose your spouse has any plans for when she accompanies you to New York?

L : She plans to visit her uncle, and she may get a job in her uncle's Chinese restaurant.

C : Are you used to American customs?

L : Not yet, but I know more than before.

C : OK. Good.

L : Thank you very much.

簽證官： 你一星期會賺多少錢？

盧先生： 我一星期應該會賺 500 元。

簽證官： 你在美國的最終目的地是哪裡？

盧先生： 紐約。

簽證官： 你的配偶跟你一起到紐約之後，有任何計劃嗎？

盧先生： 她打算去拜訪她叔叔，而且她可能會在她叔叔的中國餐館找個工作。

簽證官： 你習慣美國的風俗嗎？

盧先生： 還沒習慣，但是我比以前更了解美國了。

簽證官： 好，很好。

盧先生： 非常謝謝你。

Interview for Emigration 3

> The Lin family plans to emigrate to Canada in two years, after Mr. Lin retires from his job. According to Canada's immigration law, if they want to settle down there, they have to live in that country 183 days a year. Therefore, Mrs. Lin has decided to bring her children to live in Canada this year.

(*C* : *Consular official* *L* : *Mrs. Lin*)

L : Good morning.

C : Morning, Mrs. Lin. Have a seat.

C : Why would you like to settle in Canada?

L : Well, its climate and pleasant life style are the greatest attractions. Moreover, I have to consider the education of my son and my daughter. I think that the learning environment in Canada is better than what we have in Taiwan.

C : How about your husband? Will he come with you?

L : No, he won't. He needs to wait until he retires from his job.

移民面談 3

林家打算在兩年後移民到加拿大，也就是在林先生退休之後。而根據加拿大的移民法，如果要在那邊定居，則他們一年內必須在加拿大住滿 183 天。因此，林太太決定今年要帶著孩子們到加拿大住。

（*C*：簽證官　*L*：林太太）

林太太： 早安。

簽證官： 早安，林太太。請坐。

簽證官： 妳為什麼想要在加拿大定居？

林太太： 嗯，加拿大的氣候和愉快的生活方式，是最吸引人的地方。除此之外，我還得考慮我兒子和女兒的教育。我認為加拿大的教育環境比台灣好。

簽證官： 那妳先生呢？他會跟你們一起去嗎？

林太太： 不，他不會。他必須等到退休之後。

C : What kind of job does your husband do?

L : He is a marketing executive in K.S. Corporation, and that company is one of the biggest recreational vehicle companies in Taiwan.

C : Can you show me your financial statement?

L : OK. Let me open it for you.

C : What would you do after you emigrate to Canada? How will you get a job at your age?

L : Well, actually, I'm not planning to search for a job there. My husband and I would like to open a grocery store. And with our savings and retirement pension, I don't think we will have any problem living in Canada.

C : What did you do in Taiwan before?

L : I was an English teacher in a high school.

C : Have you been to Canada before?

L : Yes, I've been there several times. You know, I had to find out about the life style and the customs there, so that we can get used to our new environment as soon as possible.

C : That's fine. I'll issue you a visa, but you have to wait some time.

L : How long must I wait?

C : Maybe one week.

L : Thank you very much. Have a nice day!

簽證官： 妳先生從事什麼工作？

林太太： 他在 K.S.公司擔任行銷主管，而該公司是台灣最大的休旅車公司之一。

簽證官： 可以看一下妳的財力證明嗎？

林太太： 沒問題。我拿給你看。

簽證官： 妳移民到加拿大之後要做什麼？以妳的年紀要怎麼找到工作呢？

林太太： 嗯，實際上，我不打算在那裡找工作。我先生和我想開一家雜貨店。而且以我們的存款和退休金，我覺得要在加拿大生活是沒有問題的。

簽證官： 妳以前在台灣從事什麼行業？

林太太： 我在高中當英文老師。

簽證官： 妳以前去過加拿大嗎？

林太太： 去過，我去過很多次。你知道的，我必須觀察一下那裡的生活型態和習俗，如此一來，我們才能儘快適應新環境。

簽證官： 好的，我會發簽證給妳，但是妳必須等一會兒。

林太太： 我大概要等多久？

簽證官： 可能要一星期。

林太太： 非常謝謝你。祝你有個美好的一天！

心得筆記欄

第⑥篇 ▶ 自傳・信函

Autobiography & Letter

📄 Autobiography 1

My last name is Wang and my first name is Chih-wei. I was born on February 18, 1980 in Tainan, Taiwan. There are five in my family including me and I am the eldest son. I completed elementary, junior and senior high school in Tainan. And I entered Tsing Hua University in Hsinchu in 1998. I received a bachelor's degree in computer science last year. Since that time, I have been employed as a computer engineer by the Dah Tung Company.

I've been interested in computers since I was quite young. I've been clever with my hands and even built a simple computer myself in my junior high school days. And I think there's a very good future in this precision instrument here in Taiwan, so for a long time I've been thinking I'd like to study abroad.

I would like to be admitted to your graduate school to earn an M.A. and a Ph.D. I think studying in your university would give me the best opportunity to build up more specific skills and knowledge. My ultimate goal is to become a professor and I want to contribute whatever I learn to improving technology in Taiwan.

I enclose my study plan and a letter of recommendation from my university professor. I would be most grateful if you would grant me admission to your university.

📄 自 傳 1

　　我的名字是王志偉，一九八〇年二月十八日在台灣省台南市出生。我家包括我共有五個人，我是長子。我在台南唸完小學、國中、和高中。一九九八年進入新竹的清華大學就讀，去年得到資訊工程學士學位。此後我一直受聘爲大同公司的電腦工程師。

　　我從小就對電腦感興趣。我的手很靈巧，國中的時候甚至替自己組了一部簡單的電腦。我想這種精密儀器在台灣這裡的遠景十分看好，所以我長久以來都一直想要去留學。

　　我想進入貴校的研究所攻讀碩士和博士學位。我認爲在貴校唸書，能給我最好的機會，來增進更多專門技能與知識。我最終的目標是要成一位教授，並貢獻所學來提昇台灣的科技。

　　我附上我的研究計畫和一封我大學教授的推薦函。如能獲准進入貴校就讀，我將非常感激。

** ————————————————

last name 姓 (= *family name* = *surname* (ˈsɝ͵nem))
first name 名　　　***bachelor's degree*** 學士學位
precision (prɪˈsɪʒən) *n.* 精密；精確
precision instrument 精密儀器
ultimate (ˈʌltəmɪt) *adj.* 最終的
see ~ through 對 ~ 負責到底
enclose (ɪnˈkloz) *v.* (隨函) 附寄
grateful (ˈgretfəl) *adj.* 感激的　　grant (grænt) *v.* 給予
admission (ədˈmɪʃən) *n.* 入學許可

📄 Autobiography 2

AUTOBIOGRAPHY
by Yao-Ting Lin

I was born in Taichung, Taiwan. I received all my education there, beginning with primary school almost twenty years ago and concluding with my graduation this June from National Chung Hsing University.

From the time I start to specialize in the field of economics, I made continuous progress in all branches of economic science. I took an active part in classroom discussions, which greatly increased my understanding of economics.

I also gained worthwhile results as a result of my research work. Due to my hard work, I obtained very high grades each semester and these earned me several scholarships.

After graduation I took a job working at the Bank of America in Taipei. I worked there for two years.

I feel strongly that Taiwan needs better-educated men. I would like to accomplish something good for my own country and do what I enjoy most.

At present I am eager to be admitted to your graduate school to obtain a master's degree and later a Ph. D.

I hope you will allow me to strive toward the fulfillment of my ambitions through advanced studies at your university.

Thank you very much.

自傳 2

自傳

林耀庭

　　我生於台灣省台中市。我在那裡接受所有的教育，從大約二十年前，開始上小學，到今年六月自國立中興大學畢業為止。

　　從我開始專攻經濟學起，我就不斷地涉獵與經濟學有關的各門學科。我積極參與課堂討論，並因此而大幅增進自己對經濟學的了解。

　　我在研究工作上也有具體的成果。由於我的努力，我每學期都得到很好的成績，還因此獲得了幾種獎學金。

　　畢業後，我在台北的美國銀行工作。我在那裡待了兩年。

　　我深深覺得台灣需要學養更豐富的人。我希望能對自己的國家有所貢獻，同時做自己最喜歡的事。

　　目前我渴望獲准進入貴校研究所拿碩士學位，然後再拿博士學位。

　　我希望您能允許我經由在貴校的深造，而得以努力實現我的抱負。

　　非常感謝您。

** ————————————————

conclude with 以～作為結束

specialize〔'spɛʃəlˌaɪz〕*v.* 專攻 < *in* >

branch〔bræntʃ〕*n.* 分支

📑 Autobiography 3

My name is Hung Jui-chuai. I was born on June 10, 1971. I lived in Kaohsiung until I graduated from high school. I entered the Department of Chinese Literature of National Taiwan University in 1989. And because of that, I moved to Taipei. After I got my bachelor's degree in Chinese Literature, I found a job at Elle magazine as a column editor.

My parents are both teachers; one of them teaches in junior high school, and the other one teaches at Chang Gung Institute of Technology. Since I was very young, they have encouraged me to read as many books as possible. Therefore, one of my biggest hobbies is reading books. When I read, if I find something interesting in that book, I will feel very happy. So after I graduated from university, I decided to be a creative and humorous writer. And that's why I've worked for Elle magazine for eight years.

I quit that job last year, because I think I need to learn something new. I hope you can consider me as a position as lecturer in the Chinese Literature Department. I'm confident that I can teach students something different about practical writing. I believe my work experience can be a big help in teaching. Thank you for your kind attention.

📄 自 傳 3

　　我的名字是洪瑞川。生於一九七一年六月十日。高中畢業之前都住在高雄。我於一九八九年,進入國立台灣大學中文系就讀。也因此而搬到台北。在拿到中文系的學士學位之後,我在 Elle 雜誌找到一份專欄編輯的工作。

　　我的父母都是老師,其中一個在國中教書,另一個則是在長庚技術學院教書。他們從小就鼓勵我讀越多書越好。因此,我最大的嗜好之一,就是讀書。當我閱讀時,如果能從書中得到有趣的啟發,我就會覺得非常開心。所以在我大學畢業之後,我就決定要當一個有創意而幽默的作家。而這也是我在 Elle 雜誌工作了八年的原因。

　　我在去年辭掉了那份工作,因為我覺得我需要學一些新的東西。希望您可以考慮讓我來擔任中文系的講師一職。我有信心能在實際寫作方面,給予學生不同的指導方向。我想我的工作經驗對教學會有很大的幫助。謝謝您的關照。

**

chamber (ˈtʃembɚ) *n.* 房間
column (ˈkɑləm) *n.* 專欄　　quit (kwɪt) *v.* 辭職
lecturer (ˈlɛktʃərɚ) *n.* 講師

📇 Resume 1

Name : Yang Wen-che
Date of Birth : July 25, 1974
Permanent Address : 22 Sinyi Road, Section 3, Keelung
Present Address : 100, Ren-ai Road, Section 1, Taipei
Telephone : 2878-0584

EDUCATION

July 1992   Graduated from Chien Kuo High School, Taipei

September, 1992   Entered Cheng Kung University, Tainan

June 1996   Graduated from the Cheng Kung University

June 2001   Received an MBA from Cheng Chi University, Taipei

WORK EXPERIENCE

Since October 2001   Employed as a marketing assistant by the Dah Tung Trading Company, Taipei

履歷表 1

姓　　名：楊文哲
生　　日：1974 年 7 月 25 日
永久地址：基隆市信義路三段 22 號
現在地址：台北市仁愛路一段 100 號
電　　話：2878-0584

學　　歷

| 1992 年 7 月 | 畢業於台北建國中學 |

1992 年 7 月　　　　　　畢業於台北建國中學

1992 年 9 月　　　　　　進入台南成功大學就讀

1996 年 6 月　　　　　　畢業於成功大學

2001 年 6 月　　　　　　在台北的政治大學得到企管碩士
　　　　　　　　　　　　學位

工作經驗

自 2001 年 10 月起　　　受聘爲台北大通貿易公司的行銷
　　　　　　　　　　　　助理

MILITARY SERVICE

August 1996   Enlisted in the army as a private

June 1998   Discharged from service and
placed on the reserve list

AWARDS

Award :   Awarded the third prize in the
College English Speech Contest
in October, 1994

I affirm that the above statements are true and correct
in every respect.
August 15, 2003

兵 役

1996 年 8 月	應召入伍當兵
1998 年 6 月	退伍，名列後備軍人名冊

獎 項

獎：	1994 年 10 月得到大專英語演講比賽第三名

我確認上述各項為真，且正確無誤。

2003 年 8 月 15 日

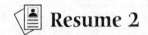

Resume 2

Jung-kuo Wang

4th Fl., 35 Ren-ai Rd., Sec.2, Taipei

(02) 2955-3993

POSITION SOUGHT

System operator in electronics company, preferably in Hsinchu City.

EDUCATION

Bachelor of Science, Tsing Hua University, 1998

EXPERIENCE

From July, 2000 to present, I have been employed as a computer engineer at LP Technology, Inc. I made several suggestions to maintain the computer systems in our company which proved to be so effective.

PERSONAL

Age 28, 178cm, 82kg. Excellent health. Completed military service. Singled. Active in baseball and mountain climbing.

履歷表 2

王戎國
台北市仁愛路二段 35 號 4 樓
（02）2955-3993

應徵職位

電子公司的系統管理員，地點以新竹市為佳。

教育程度

1998 年拿到清華大學理學士學位

經　歷

從 2000 年 7 月至今，在 LP 科技公司擔任電腦工程師。曾對公司的電腦系統維護提出幾項建議，結果都非常有效。

個人資料

28 歲，178 公分，82 公斤。健康狀況極佳。役畢。單身。興趣是棒球和爬山。

LICENSES

Driver's license and class B technician's certificate.

LANGUAGES

Fluent in Mandarin and English.

SALARY

According to your salary scale.

REFERENCE

My present supervisor — Mr. Tsai Tsung-hsun, who will be glad to talk about my work experience with you via phone: 2955-9363.

證　　照

駕照和乙級技術士證照。

語　　言

中英文流利。

薪　　資

依公司規定。

推薦人

我目前的上司 —— 蔡宗勳先生，他會很樂意和您談論
我的工作經歷，請電洽 2955-9363。

✉ Application Letter 1

Dear Sir,

Since I hope to further my studies in the United States, I would like to enter your graduate school of Sociology for the fall semester of 2004. I would appreciate your sending me the necessary application forms for admission and financial support for an master degree in sociology.

All my credentials will be forwarded to you. I am looking forward to hearing from you soon.

Sincerely yours,

Cheng Fu-Ming

Cheng Fu-Ming

申請書 1

敬啟者：

　　因為我希望到美國深造，所以我想進貴校 2004 年秋季班的社會學研究所。如蒙惠寄必備的入學申請表，並得到貴校對攻讀社會學碩士學位的資助，將非常感謝。

　　我會寄上所有的資格證明書，盼望能很快得到您的消息。

　　　　　　　　　　　　　　　　　陳福明　敬上

＊＊────────────

further ('fɜðɚ) v. 促進；深造
sociology (ˌsoʃɪ'ɑlədʒɪ) n. 社會學
admission (əd'mɪʃən) n. 准許進入
credential (krɪ'dɛnʃəl) n. 證明書
forward ('fɔrwɚd) v. 轉寄

✉ Application Letter 2

Dear Virginia Scholarship Committee,

Please consider my application for the Virginia Scholarship. Enclosed are the completed application form and a letter of recommendation from my principal. I am a self-supporting student.

The scholarship qualifications call for students who stand out in the classroom as well as in the community. My academic success, as well as my extracurricular activities makes me a good candidate for the said scholarship.

Academically, I maintain an overall 3.7 GPA. I am also the current president of the college's Biology Club. As president, I provide direction for our club's activities and projects. This year we successfully held an exhibit showcasing endangered species and what steps are being taken to ensure their continued existence. I am also drawing up the details of our upcoming Inter-School Science Contest to be held early next year. I contribute weekly articles to our college newspaper and give regular speeches to Girl/Boy Scout troops.

申請書 2

維吉尼亞獎學金委員會敬啟：

　　請將我的申請列入維吉尼亞獎學金的候選名單中。隨函附寄的是完整的申請表格，還有校長的推薦函。我是個自費生。

　　這個獎學金是發給具有某些資格的學生，他們必須在課堂和社團的表現都十分出色。而我在學業上的成就，和在課外活動中的表現，都使我有資格成為這個獎學金的優秀候選人。

　　在學業上，我的總平均一直都維持在 3.7。我在我目前就讀的那所大學，還擔任生物社的社長。身為社長，我必須指揮社團活動和計劃的進行。今年我們成功地舉辦了一場瀕臨絕種的動植物櫥窗展覽，而且還成功地採取一些步驟，使它們能繼續生存下去。我目前正在為明年年初即將舉辦的校際科展規劃細節。我每個星期都投稿到學校的報社，而且會定期為女童軍團和男童軍團演講。

My father passed away two years ago, and as the oldest of five siblings from a single-parent family, I am supporting myself through college. Receiving this scholarship will greatly reduce my financial burden.

Thank you for considering my application.

Sincerely,

Jane Keats

Jane Keats

　　我父親兩年前去世了，來自單親家庭，且身爲五個兄弟姊妹中最年長的我，必須負擔自己的大學學費。如果能申請到這份獎學金，將會大爲減輕我的經濟負擔。

感謝您將我的申請列入考慮。

珍‧濟慈　敬上

**

enclose（ ɪn'kloz ）v.（隨函）附寄

principal（ 'prɪnsəpḷ ）n. 校長

self-supporting（ ˌsɛlfsə'portɪŋ ）adj. 自食其力的

qualifications（ ˌkwɑləfə'keʃənz ）n. pl. 資格

call for 需要；要求　　*stand out* 傑出

as well as 以及　　community（ kə'mjunətɪ ）n. 社團

extracurricular（ ˌɛkstrəkə'rɪkjələ ）adj. 課外的

candidate（ 'kændəˌdet ）n. 候選人

said（ sɛd ）adj. 前述的；上述的

GPA 學業成績總平均（ = *grade point average* ）

showcase（ 'ʃoˌkes ）v. 把…放在展示櫥櫃內

endangered species 瀕臨絕種的動植物

draw up 草擬　　upcoming（ 'ʌpˌkʌmɪŋ ）adj. 即將來臨的

scout（ skaʊt ）n. 童子軍　　troop（ trup ）n. 團

pass away 去世　　sibling（ 'sɪblɪŋ ）n. 兄弟姊妹

Letter of Recommendation 1

January 10, 2004

To whom it may concern:

I understand that Miss Li-hsin Lee has applied to your university and am herewith providing a recommendation for her.

Our university has a history of approximately eighty years with special emphasis on law. Entrance competition is high with only one successful applicant out of over ten. Miss Lee is a graduate of such a faculty of law.

She was one of my undergraduate students, graduating with a bachelor's degree in law in June 2002, and I feel that I know the applicant very well. In my class we discussed social sciences in general in the first year and more specific topics in the second year. She digested all these subjects thoroughly, participated in class activities and expressed creative and thoughtful views.

Concerning personality, Miss Lee is superficially quiet and passive but is actually full of pleasant aggressiveness, abhorring easy compromise. Her positive scholastic attitude and life style have helped her execute important business responsibilities in the business circles here, first with Hsin Huang Co., a real estate company. She controlled their contracts from July 2002 through September 2003. Secondly she was employed by Sung Wei Trading Company in their planning section from October 2003 to date.

推薦函 1

2004 年 1 月 10 日

敬啓者：

　　我知道李麗馨小姐已向貴校申請入學，所以我在此爲她寫一封推薦函。

　　敝校特重法律，約有八十年的歷史，入學考試競爭激烈，十多人中，才錄取一人，李小姐就是這樣一所法學院的畢業生。

　　她是我大學部的學生之一，2002 年 6 月畢業時拿到法學士學位，所以我覺得我非常了解這位申請人。我的課程第一年是概括地討論社會科學，第二年則討論較專門的主題。她能徹底地了解這些主題，參與課堂活動，並提出了有創意而深入的見解。

　　在個性方面，李小姐表面上是安靜而被動的，但實際上卻充滿了和善的進取精神，並痛恨輕易妥協。她積極的求學態度與生活方式，使她在此地的商業界中，擔任重要的商業職務，她首先是在新皇 ── 一家房地產公司任職。她負責管理該公司的契約，從 2002 年 7 月到 2003 年 9 月；繼而受聘於松偉貿易公司企劃部，從 2003 年 10 月迄今。

I gather Miss Lee now wants to tackle advanced studies in business in the United States, using the business experience she gained here. I am convinced that she will do a good job in her new pursuit and have no hesitation in recommending Miss Lee to you.

Your serious consideration of this applicant will be appreciated.

Yours sincerely,

(Dr.) Liu Jen-kuang

Professor of Political Science

　　我推想李小姐現在是想應用她在這裡所得到的商業經
驗，到美國做更深入的商業研究。我相信她在她的新研究
上，會表現得很出色，所以毫不猶豫地向您推薦李小姐。

　　我將非常感激您對這位申請人所做的鄭重考慮。

　　　　　　　　　　政治學教授

　　　　　　　　　　劉任光（博士）　敬上

** ————————————————

herewith〔hɪr'wɪθ〕adv.（隨函）附寄
faculty〔'fækl̩tɪ〕n. 學院
undergraduate〔ˌʌndɚ'grædʒʊɪt〕n. 大學部在校生
digest〔daɪ'dʒɛst〕v. 理解
concerning〔kən'sɜnɪŋ〕prep. 關於
superficially〔ˌsupɚ'fɪʃəlɪ〕adv. 表面上
aggressiveness〔ə'grɛsɪvnɪs〕n. 積極進取
abhor〔əb'hɔr〕v. 痛恨
scholastic〔sko'læstɪk〕adj. 學問上的
execute〔'ɛksɪˌkjut〕v. 執行；完成
business circle 商業界　　**real estate** 房地產
to date 迄今　　gather〔'gæðɚ〕v. 推測
tackle〔'tækl̩〕v. 認眞著手
pursuit〔pɚ'sut〕n. 從事的事；研究

Letter of Recommendation 2

February 1, 2004

To whom it may concern:

It is with a great pleasure that I recommend Lin Wei-chung to your company.

From my observation during the four-year period I taught him at college, I can assure you that Mr. Lin is not only an ardent worker but also a trustworthy man. He has a marvelous command of practical English, both written and spoken, and also a strong sense of responsibility. And he is always agreeable and gets along well with other students.

I feel confident that he will prove an invaluable help to your company if you employ him.

Yours sincerely,
Wang Chun-ming
Professor, Chiao Tung
University

推薦函 2

2004 年 2 月 1 日

敬啓者：

我很榮幸向貴公司推薦林維中。

從我大學四年教他時所做的觀察，我可以向您保證，林先生不但是個熱心工作的人，也是一個值得信賴的人。他非常精通實用英語，包括說和寫，而且有強烈的責任感。他一向都很和善，跟其他學生也處得很好。

如果您聘用他，我相信他對貴公司而言，會是個極重要的助力。

交通大學教授

王俊明　敬上

**

ardent（ˈɑrdn̩t）*adj.* 熱心的
trustworthy（ˈtrʌstˌwɜðɪ）*adj.* 可信賴的
command（kəˈmænd）*n.*（對語言）運用自如的能力
agreeable（əˈgriəbl̩）*adj.* 討人喜歡的；和藹的
invaluable（ɪnˈvæljəbl̩）*adj.* 非常寶貴的

 Letter of Recommendation 3

Mr. George C. Johnson,
Department of Economics,
University of Southern California

Dear Sir:

This is to recommend to you Mr. Chung-ping Chou, who will soon graduate from National Sun Yat-Sen University.

I rarely recommend a student to a foreign university unless I am convinced that he will be able to perform well and be a credit to his country. Mr. Chou, as one of the best students in this university, is worthy of being recommended.

Mr. Chou has shown a high degree of maturity performing well at a foreign university. In addition, he has a very good command of the English language.

As his professor from 2001 to 2004, I feel myself qualified to comment on many aspects of his character. If I can be of any future aid to you in the processing of Mr. Chou's application, please do not hesitate to notify me.

Sincerely yours,
Yen Hsiao-wen
Professor of Economics

推薦函 3

南加大經濟學系
喬治‧強森先生

敬啓者：

　　我在此向您推薦周忠平先生，他即將從國立中山大學畢業。

　　我很少向國外的大學推薦學生，除非我深信他能學有所成，並爲國增光。周先生是這所大學最優秀的學生之一，值得向您推薦。

　　周先生已顯示出具有在國外大學唸好書的優秀能力。此外，他非常精通英文。

　　從 2001 年到 2004 年擔任他的教授，我覺得自己很適合評論他個性中的許多層面。如果我能在您處理周先生的申請上有任何幫助，請立即通知我，不必遲疑。

經濟學教授
顏孝文　敬上

**

credit〔ˋkrɛdɪt〕 *n.* 光榮
maturity〔məˋtjʊrətɪ〕 *n.* 成熟；完備
command〔kəˋmænd〕 *n.* （對語言）運用自如的能力

第 ⑦ 篇 ▶ 補充資料

More Information

第一章 企管類研究所

　　企管類研究所包括國企所、國貿所、商研所、企管所、科管所、管研所、經管所、管科所、人資所、行銷所，總計十大系所，因為二十一世紀是商業與科技並駕齊驅的時代，所以企管類研究所的涵蓋範圍非常廣泛。而欲甄試該類研究所的考生為數眾多，但錄取人數十分有限，所以競爭非常激烈。推甄成功與否，一般是看學業成績及口試表現，只要學業成績達一定標準，那麼如何在口試時表現得沉穩而出色，就成了最重要的關鍵。以下將分別介紹，企管類研究所的英文口試常考試題、中文口試常考試題與相關注意事項：

■ 第1部份　英文口試常考試題

1. 英文自我介紹

【範例①】(30秒)

　　Good morning. My name is Huang Chao-tang and I live in Taipei. Now I'm a student in the Public Finance Department in Chengchi University. I like reading newspapers and watching movies. I'm also a member of tennis club. My father is a regional manager for Ta-tung Electronic Company, and my mother is a housewife. We often go on a picnic on weekends. My favorite subject in college is business administration, because I consider it a challenging course. I hope that I'll have the opportunity to pursue advanced knowledge in this subject.

早安。我的名字是黃昭塘，我住在台北。我目前是政治大學財政系的學生。我喜歡看報紙和看電影。我還是網球社的社員。我父親是大通電子公司的區域經理，而我母親則是家庭主婦。我們週末常會去野餐。我大學時最喜歡的科目是企業管理，因爲我認爲那是一門具有挑戰性的學科。我希望能有機會追求這門科目裡更高深的知識。

【範例 2】(1-2 分鐘；考生可依自己的課內外成就，加以補充)

Good afternoon. My name is Huang Chao-tang, and I live in Taipei city. I like to go swimming and play basketball with my friends. My father and mother are both government officials. They always encourage me to study hard and read as many books as I can. Now I'm a graduate of Chengchi University. I majored in public finance. I was the leader of the student club in our department, and we won the right to choose our own tutor during my administration. Furthermore, as a public finance major, I have taken courses in business administration, international trade, management, and financial management. I am really interested in business administration and hope to pursue advanced studies in this subject. My personal goal is to be a professional manager in the future, so I think that I need to learn as much as I can about this field. I think that knowing how to take advantage of manpower and resources is the most important thing to an outstanding management. I believe your department can give me the best opportunity to learn.

午安。我的名字是黃昭塘，我住在台北市。我喜歡游泳還有和朋友一起打籃球。我爸媽都是公務員。他們總是鼓勵我用功讀書，和讀愈多書愈好。我是政大畢業生，主修財政。我曾經擔任財政系的學生會會長，而且在我的任期內，我們取得了選擇導師的權力。此外，因為主修財政，所以我還修了企業管理、國際貿易、管理學和財務管理的課程。我對企管真的很有興趣，而且希望可以在這個學科內追求更高深的學問。我個人的目標，是在未來成為一個專業的管理人才，所以我認為我應該在這個領域內，盡我所能地學習。我認為對於一位出色的管理者而言，知道如何善用人力以及資源，是最重要的。而我相信貴所能給我最佳的學習機會。

2. 基本英文對話能力測試。(會根據自我介紹的內容出題，可能問及求學過程、打工經歷或大學時最喜歡的科目…等。請參考本書第一篇和第三篇)

3. Please describe your ability in research.
   請說明你的研究能力。

4. Why do you think that you should be accepted by this school? Do you have any special advantages?
   你為什麼認為自己可以進入本所？你有任何特別的優點嗎？

5. What's your career goal after graduating from this school?
   你畢業之後的生涯規劃為何？

6. Do you have any special accomplishments?
   你有任何特殊才藝嗎？

7. To which field do you think your character is best suited in the five management? (Human Resource Management, Information Management, Operation and Production Management, Finance Management or Marketing Management)
你覺得你的特質跟「五管」中哪個領域最相稱？（人力資源管理、資訊管理、作業與生產管理、財務管理或行銷管理）

8. Please comment on your learning ability and creativity.
試評論你的學習能力和創造力。

9. How can the relationship between Taiwan and China be improved?
如何改善兩岸的關係？

10. What's the difference between Taiwan and Korea in approach to branding? You may use Samsung as an example.
台灣在品牌方面與南韓有何不同？可以三星為例。

11. What's your opinion on Taiwanese investment in China?
對於台商赴大陸投資，你的看法為何？

12. What's your future goal? How will you accomplish that?
你未來的目標是什麼？要怎麼完成它？

13. How do you balance your job with your family responsibility?
你如何平衡事業與家庭責任？

14. Why do you think you are chosen for an interview?
你認為你為什麼會被選中前來面試？

15. If you encounter some ambiguous situation or you feel under stress when you're carrying out your research, what will you do to resolve that?
如果你在做研究時，遇到模稜兩可的狀況或覺得壓力很大，你會如何解決？

16. Please tell me your opinion on the ups and downs of the Internet industry and the burst of the Internet bubble.
對於網路企業的興衰與泡沫化，請提出你的看法。

17. Who is the most memorable person in your mind?
你記憶中最難忘的人是誰？

18. Which characteristics do you have that are correspondent to those of an MBA student?
你認為自己有哪些特質符合一個 MBA 的學生？

19. What is green marketing?
何謂綠色行銷？

20. Which native enterprise do you like best? Why?
你最喜歡哪一個本土企業？為什麼？

21. Why did you choose this university?
你為什麼選擇這所大學？

22. Which male entrepreneur do you admire most? Why?
你最欣賞的男性企業家是誰？為什麼？

23. Which female entrepreneur do you admire most?
    Why? 你最欣賞的女性企業家是誰？爲什麼？

24. What do you think is the most serious problem for
    Taiwan?
    你認爲目前台灣最嚴重的問題是什麼？

25. Mr. Chang Chung-mou said that young people should
    have foresight and goals, and not just think about
    making money. What do you think about that?
    張忠謀說年輕人要有遠見和目標，不要光想賺錢，你認
    爲呢？

26. In your opinion, what kind of principles should a good
    enterprise have?
    你覺得一個好的企業應具備哪些準則？

27. After Taiwan joined WTO, what kind of opportunities
    has Taiwan had to compete with other countries?
    台灣加入 WTO 之後，有何機會能與其他國家競爭？

28. What kind of leadership skills do you have？Please
    give me a real example.
    你認爲你具備何種領導技巧？請舉出實例。

29. Since Taiwan has joined the WTO, should we change our
    management approach?
    加入 WTO 之後，我們應該改變任何管理方法嗎？

第2部份 中文口試常考試題

第一節 一般企管類研究所

1. 簡單的自我介紹
   (1) 個性、優缺點、興趣、未來的抱負。
   (2) 工作經驗、社團經驗。
   (3) 求學過程、最喜歡的科目、最難的科目、大學修過哪些課程、有修過數學方面的課嗎、大學聯考數學分數、在校排名如何？
   (4) 印象最深刻的事、最令你沮喪的事、目前最關心的事、最自豪的事、如何克服你認為最困難的事。（舉例說明）
   (5) 服務公司或就讀學校的環境。

2. 報考該科研究所的動機。（沒有報考母校研究所的原因；一共報名了幾所學校的甄試？其異同為何；為什麼不先投入就業市場，再回頭進修；針對跨系考生，在校習得的知識如何運用在企業管理的研究上）

3. 為什麼馬路上的蓋子多是圓形的？請舉出三個理由。

4. 你認為你們系上的學生，相較於管院其他系所的學生有什麼特質？

5. 未來研究方向。（企管的範圍極廣，未來將專注於哪個研究方向，研究主題、研究計劃為何）

6. 為什麼要用 XX 產業當作專題，你對它未來在台灣的發展有什麼看法？

7. 人力資源管理的範疇和重要性。

8. 提出讓教授從眾多優秀考生中錄取你的充分理由。（自我推銷）

9. 談一談你在社團或班級的領導經驗。

10. 你認為你是一個 leader 還是 team member？

11. 有沒有主辦過大型活動的經驗？在這段過程裡，你如何解決人際網絡的問題，又如何在活動內容的創新與守舊之間抉擇？

12. 本所以培養專業經理人為目標，你覺得自己有什麼樣的特質可以成為專業經理人？能否舉例說明自己的領導特質。

13. 你對本校企管課程的期望為何？

14. 你會用什麼方法來激勵別人？

15. 修習經濟學的作用為何？

16. 就兩岸貿易情勢而言，台灣有何利基？

17. 你認為台灣是否應開放戒急用忍政策？

18. 你對做研究有興趣嗎？

19. 談談所從事過的研究之進行過程、研究方法與收穫。

20. 試舉一管理實例，並說明其背後的管理意義。

21. 為何留學生的比例逐年下降，請解釋其原因。

22. 本土研究生如何增進國際觀？

23. 請比較一下國內外的大學，國內大學的優勢為何？

24. 為什麼不選擇出國唸書？

25. 資訊科技對經營技術有無影響？其影響為何？

26. 資訊管理對企業管理有何幫助？

27. 將來如有餘力，會不會多修一些課程？

28. 有沒有與外國人互動的機會？頻率如何？

29. 五管中，你最有興趣的是？你認為管理是一門藝術還是科學？為什麼？

30. 將來為何想唸作業管理與行銷管理？

31. 二十一世紀是電子商務、資訊科技的時代，你認為在這個時代中，作業管理和行銷會有什麼新的議題與應用？

32. 你認為在二十一世紀中，五管裡的哪一管會是未來的趨勢？為什麼？

33. 重視顧客的行銷方法，符合那一個 C 開頭的理論？

34. 給定一篇英文短文，唸過一遍後，把大意說出來。

35. 以學生的觀點，你認為老師應該怎麼做，才能增進師生間的關係？

36. 假設現在有兩位老師，一位是專注於學術研究，對於學生活動則比較沒有時間參與；另一位是積極參與學生活動，而對學術研究則較不積極。你會選擇哪一位？為什麼？

37. 假設現在兩位老師都各自往極端發展，發揮他們最大效用，你認為這樣好嗎？

38. ERP 是什麼的縮寫，中文為何？

39. 個案題目《Where Information Is Everything》
    ⑴ 請問這篇個案在說什麼？
    ⑵ 你認為資訊真的代表一切嗎？
    ⑶ 資訊與人在管理中的優先順序為何？如何保持人與資訊的平衡？
    ⑷ 你如何利用資訊分享，來建立員工對企業的認同感？
    ⑸ 可以舉例說明分享資訊帶給顧客滿足這部分的概念嗎？
    ⑹ 如果你是高階經理人，你會如何與員工分享資訊？又會如何選擇要與員工分享哪些資訊？

40. 面對辦公室文化中的無預警裁員與購併流言，你將採用何種管理策略？

41. 唸研究所對你的前途有何助益？

42. 參加某社團的原因？是對學習有興趣？還是對人有興趣？為什麼？

43. 你印象最深刻的電影是？為何國片一直無法蓬勃發展？

44. Hollywood 成功的原因在哪裡？

45. 請針對行銷，先舉出一個課本上的理論，簡單敘述後，提出你個人的評論。請不要從實務引入，單就課本出現的理論來說明。

46. 大學時的行銷學老師是誰？用哪一本課本？課本內容為何？上課內容為何？

47. 作業管理老師是哪位？課本用哪一本？課本內容為何？上課內容為何？

48. 行銷管理與生產作業管理有何不同，二者是否有互相衝突之處？

49. 手上若有五張股票，如何作投資組合？

50. 大學時期最擅長的科目為何？該科目所使用的教科書為何？作者是誰？

51. 對經發會的看法為何？

52. 加入 WTO，對台灣的影響為何？

53. 知識經濟對傳統產業有何衝擊？

54. 對於 BBS 上同學不負責任的發言，有什麼解決的辦法？

55. 如果版主砍文章還是不能制止，那該怎麼辦？

56. 贊不贊成現在 BBS 上採用的匿名制度？

57. 請提出本校的一項缺點。

58. 你覺得台灣企業最欠缺什麼？

59. 你覺得會計對於管理有何幫助？

60. 企業家除了將利潤最大化之外，你覺得還有什麼是應該做的？

61. 請分析台北市長選舉的競選策略。（此為考古題，今年則可能考分析總統大選的競選策略。）

62. 請說出你對台灣企業發生財務金融危機的看法。

63. 本校學程制度的優缺點為何？

64. 「MBA」中的「A」為何？

65. 當家庭與事業產生衝突時，你會如何解決？

66. 請解釋為何久賭必輸？

67. 試評論今天工商時報、經濟日報的頭條。

68. 請說明你對勞工退休金年金法、個人帳戶、其他年金法的看法。

69. 你認為工作時，最重要的特質或條件是什麼？

70. 如果你將來非得從事下列工作：壽險業務員、訪員，你將如何面對工作中的挫折？

71. 你對企管的認識為何？管理涵蓋了哪些範圍？

72. 對金控公司的了解。

73. 我們學校的必修課程為何？你認為有哪些對你而言是困難的？

74. 試問一家公司如何運用策略來增加其競爭優勢？

75. 目前已考取哪些學校？如何取捨？

76. 音樂在你學習管理的過程中，給予過你什麼樣的幫助？

77. 「知識管理」和「管理知識」有何不同？

78. 如何搜尋分析股市之資訊？預測台股，有何不確定的干擾因素？

79. 試舉一併購實例。

80. 你認為台灣現階段有危機嗎？

81. 是否考過多益（TOEIC）認證？如果沒有，為什麼？如果有，是否會進一步考托福呢？

82. 除了企業管理之外，你還有哪方面的專長？

83. 請提出鉛筆的十項功能。

84. 請舉出五種企管相關雜誌。

85. 一家公司的進出口會受哪些因素影響？

86. 說明高科技產業對台灣的影響。

87. 何謂 OECD？台灣與中國大陸各列入哪個委員會？其性質各為何？

88. 何謂 OSM？

89. 歐元的發展趨勢會對台灣帶來哪些影響？

90. 請問區域性的經貿組織有哪些？其英文簡稱為何？

91. 一位優秀的國際行銷人才，需要具備什麼樣的特質？

92. 你認為管理者應該具備什麼樣的條件？

93. 行銷的核心價值是什麼？

94. 請問 CEO 的英文單字組成。

95. 試描述十年後的台灣經濟前景。

96. 試著想像並描述你畢業後的工作情形。

97. 如果你是主管，你將如何考核員工？

98. 如何提升本校的教學素質？

99. 學界如何與企業界溝通、合作？

100. 財務是什麼？

101. 就你親身接觸過的事件，請提出一個關於團隊的問題，並說明當初處理該事件的方法；另外，若就現在的觀點來看，該事件應如何解決？

102. 統一企業的宗旨為何？

103. 面對經濟不景氣，你將如何規劃你的投資計畫？

104. 何謂一流、二流、三流公司？

105. 台灣加入 WTO 後，米酒為何漲價，其對台灣經濟有何衝擊？

106. 何謂策略性思考？

107. 如果你要到中國大陸投資，你會如何規劃與執行？

第二節　科技管理所

1. 何謂品質管制？

2. 對於生技產業前景的看法為何？

3. 加入 WTO 之後，你認為你的優勢在哪裡？

4. 何謂知識管理？

5. 何謂服務業管理？

6. 你對於利率變動的趨勢有何了解？

7. 你認知中的科技管理為何？與你原本就讀的領域有何不同之處或相關之處，請個別加以說明。

8. 你們系上有哪些老師是從事與科技管理領域相關的研究？

9. 你覺得科技管理與一般的企研所有何不同？

10. 你看過哪些與科技有關的電影？

11. 對於科技產業外移有何看法？其對台灣有何衝擊？如何解決？

12. 你對「智慧財產權」的瞭解有多少？台灣目前在這方面有何發展？

13. 為何我國的生物科技產業無法起飛？

14. 試比較宏碁和台塑的組織結構和管理方法的異同。

15. 古代有所謂「士大夫不與民爭利」的說法，然而這和目前推動的「知識經濟」，是否有抵觸？

16. 如果你發現你們學校裡的圖書館編目相當混亂，根本找不到資料，你會怎麼辦？如果你剛進一家公司，卻發現裡面的傳承和資料管理相當隨便，你會如何反應？

17. 你覺得對你而言，最重要的東西是什麼？

18. 請說出你目前所遇到最大的挫折，以及你打算如何去解決。

19. 請說出一個與課業無關，但對你十分重要的興趣。

20. 試比較冬季時，濁水溪和淡水河的出海流量哪一個比較多，各為幾倍？

21. 為何台灣軟體業的發展不如硬體業？

22. 你贊成台灣與大陸進行技術轉移嗎？

23. 海峽兩岸的科技是否應該（有必要）交流？理由為何？

24. 試述最近所讀的一本科技或管理書籍，讓你印象最深刻的是哪個部分？

25. 網際網路目前的發展情況如何？周邊產業與其發展的關係為何？

26. 試述台灣的軟體產業對 MIS 有何需求？

27. 為何選考科管所而非資管所？

▌第 3 部份▌ 相關注意事項

1.【目標】台大國企所
　【注意】
　　⑴ 要能清楚且有條理地表達自己的就讀動機與意願，尤其是報考多所的考生，須有正當的理由說服口試老師。
　　⑵ 須多花時間了解該所的師資陣容。熟記教授的名字與學經歷。

2.【目標】政大企研所
　【注意】
　　口試時不分在職生與一般生，所以一般考生要特別注意，不要因為在職生的特殊表現而亂了手腳，須沉著應對。

3.【目標】交大經管所
　【注意】
　　事先充分了解該所的精神與教學目標，並在口試老師面前展現強烈的就讀意願。

4. 【目標】中央企管所
　　【注意】

(1) 會問及專業領域的問題，也就是從五管的相關研究方法問起，事先應熟讀每個領域的碩士論文至少一篇，並找時間了解各領域的大師及其著作。

(2) 會針對考生所繳交的研究報告提問，故對於自己的研究主題須非常專精，才能將話題引導至自己熟悉的領域。

(3) 避免提及過多的課外活動，該校欣賞專職學生。

5. 【目標】中山企研所
　　【注意】

(1) 英文口試為外國老師發問，故平常應多加訓練英文聽力。

(2) 多為分組口試，教授會依照小組互動情況決定是否錄取，故應以充分合作為上策。

(3) 會抽考 ICRT 相關內容，或英文報紙內容，考前可多加準備。

6. 【目標】台科大企研所
　　【注意】

該所的畢業條件為多益測驗 650 分以上，建議在甄試前先去考，可以增加自己的有利條件。

7. 【目標】雲科大企管所
　　【注意】

該所的口試題目以專業問題和時事為主，考前必須特別注意與所學相關的新聞議題。

8. 【目標】暨南貿研所
　　【注意】

該校會事先查明考生報考的所有系所，所以若口試老師問及是否有報考其他學校，務必要誠實回答，且須先準備好能說服口試老師的理由。

第二章　財金類研究所

　　由於國內經濟的蓬勃發展,加上政府致力於國際化及自由化,使得台灣對財金專業人才的需求與日俱增。財金類研究所可以提供學生專業領域的基礎訓練,畢業之後的出路則以金控公司、證券、銀行、保險和投顧公司為主。金控公司是台灣目前的最新潮流,其業務範圍涵蓋甚廣,大為提升就業市場對於財金專業人才的需求。其他像證券業和銀行等相關產業,也隨著台灣經濟發展而大為拓展其事業版圖,財金人才在市場上一直都維持著高人一等的身價,是以有志報考財金類研究所的考生,需要付出的努力也特別多,除了熟記專業領域的知識,還要能廣泛涉獵相關新聞議題,才能穩操勝券。以下將列出推甄財金類研究所時,英文口試常考試題、中文口試常考試題,與相關注意事項:

第1部份　英文口試常考試題

1. Self-introduction　英文自我介紹（相關範例請參閱企管類研究所）

2. What's your hobby?
   你的嗜好是什麼?

3. Why are you applying for graduate school?
   為什麼要考研究所?

4. What's your study plan for the future?
   你未來的研究計劃為何?

5. Do you think that with your technical background, there is any help in studying finance?
   你認為你的學術背景,對唸財務有什麼幫助?

6. Tell me your attitude toward the acquisition of a company.
   (A company bought B company and merged with it.)
   告訴我你對企業併購的看法。(A 公司買下 B 公司，且將其合併。)

7. What's your outlook on Internet business? What kind of change will it bring to financial administration?
   你對於電子商務有何看法？其對財管會造成什麼樣的變動？

8. Why do you choose to study in a domestic graduate school instead of studying abroad or finding a job?
   為什麼選擇唸國內的研究所，而不出國唸書，或找工作？

9. In addition to knowledge, what do you think will you need to be a successful manager?
   你認為要成為一個成功的經理人，除了知識之外，還要具備什麼條件？

10. When you have a difference of opinion with your boss, what will you do?
    當你和老板意見不同時，你會怎麼辦？

11. What's your future plan? How will you accomplish that?
    你如何規劃未來的生涯？要如何達成？

12. Why do you choose this college?
    你為什麼選擇這所大學？

13. What are the differences and similarities between finance and economy? 財務金融與經濟有何異同？

14. After Taiwan joined the WTO, what happened?
    台灣加入 WTO 之後，有什麼改變？

15. How will you make use of what you learn in the future?
　　未來你將如何學以致用？

■ 第 **2** 部份　中文口試常考試題

1. 針對個人相關資料發問
　(1) 最大的優缺點、個人能力評估、家庭背景。
　(2) 你遇到過最令你難過的事。
　(3) 社團經驗與收穫、課餘休閒活動、如何妥善安排讀書時間
　　　與社團活動、是否有任何工作經驗？
　(4) 哪個科目最差，為什麼？大學時的修課情形？曾交過的學
　　　期報告？未來的研究主題？
　(5) 有什麼特殊技能？會不會寫程式？

2. 請敘述一下報考動機，然後詳述自己值得被錄取的原因。

3. 總共報了幾家？各是什麼系所？

4. 唸本組需要具備很強的數理能力，你可以勝任嗎？

5. 你說你想要針對某個領域做深入的研究，那××所也可以，為
　什麼不唸××所？

6. 如果未被錄取，下一步的計劃為何？

7. 你將如何在財金領域中，充分發揮大學所學的知識？
　（非本系生）

8. 未來的生涯規劃為何？未來想從事何種工作？

9. 我國加入 WTO 後，對你的生涯規劃有何影響？（請用 3 分鐘
　敘述 WTO 對你的衝擊）

10. 就知識經濟及網路經濟擇一表達看法。

11. AMC（資產管理公司）的引進對台灣經濟的影響。

12. 你認為合理的股價應是多少？

13. 你認為外來匯率應是多少？

14. 對於恩龍事件的看法。

15. 你的投資策略為何？

16. 如果你是公司管理當局，你會如何投資？

17. 如果你是基金經理人，將採用何種投資策略？與 CAPM 有何關係？

18. 標會時，應如何定價才容易得標？標會與哪個財務理論有關？

19. 統計學專業問題，主題為 Random Variable vs. Sample Space。

20. 經濟學專業問題，主題為 Econometric Structural Form vs. Econometric Reduced Form。

21. 你對成功的定義是什麼？

22. 社會對成功的定義是什麼？當你對於成功的看法與社會的看法發生衝突時，你將如何抉擇？

23. 對於哪位老師的課印象最深刻？

24. 何謂凱因斯基本心理法則？其檢驗方法為何？

25. 對政治有何看法？

26. 你對於興票案有什麼看法？你覺得是李登輝說謊還是宋楚瑜？總統選舉會投給誰？為什麼？

27. 播放英文投影片，內容不一定連貫，可能少一段話或少幾句話，先請考生朗讀一遍，然後再用兩、三句話將主旨說出。

28. 有無任何金融相關證照？若有的話，其對你的影響為何？

29. 今天的道瓊工業指數是多少？Nasdaq（那斯達克）指數是多少？台股指數是多少？成交量多少？

30. 請對國內財金現況作一評論。

31. 請分析一下台灣未來的前景，以及台灣股市的前景。

32. 試分析台灣股市的中、長期趨勢。

33. 請問台商到大陸投資，政府應如何控管資金外流的問題？

34. 說明台股與美股的未來走勢，其理由為何？

35. 台灣景氣的展望與美國的關聯。

36. 政府最應採行哪些政策，以拯救台灣經濟？

37. 有關企業購併，應如何衡量企業的價值？

38. 統一超商要與博客來書店合併，應如何衡量博客來的價值？

39. 品牌的價值如何衡量？

40. 期貨價格如何決定？

41. 台灣有期貨交易嗎？交易量多少？有什麼商品？

42. 期貨與選擇權有什麼異同？

43. 某某投資評估案在評價時有哪些特別的考量因素？

44. 試算價格為多少？最後成交價是多少？

45. 該案有無運用到實質選擇權？何為實質選擇權？又應如何運用？

46. WTO 對於金融業的影響為何？

47. 加入 WTO，對哪些金融行業來說，其發展較有利？對哪些金融行業來說，弊大於利？你的看法為何？

48. 911 事件對保險業有何影響。

49. 台灣的生死合險市佔率有多少？

50. 什麼是責任準備金？

51. VAR 全名為何？

52. 修過哪些統計課程？

53. 修過哪些財金課程？在財金類課程中，哪一科令你印象最深刻，為什麼？

54. 你對銀行逾放比過高的看法。

55. NPV＝0 的專案，是否應該接受？

56. 為何聯電和台積電在美國發行的 ADR 和台灣的股票之間會有溢價？

57. 如果你可以到月球渡假，你最想帶哪三本書？為什麼？

58. 迴歸的基本意義為何？

59. 短期匯率與長期匯率是否具有相關性？如何檢定？

60. SAS 程式之應用。

61. 資本市場與貨幣市場的區別。

62. 在統計分配中，何種分配具有對稱性質？

63. 你會使用哪些統計軟體？

64. 對於台灣認購權證的價格過高，你有什麼看法？

65. 相關係數是什麼？相關係數高，是否表示有因果關係？

66. G8 高峰會有哪幾國？

67. 金控公司對臺灣的影響為何？

68. 請評估你的外語能力、數理能力和電腦能力。

69. 請說明台灣最近發生金融危機的原因。

70. 何謂指數？那是代表什麼意思？

71. 「隨機」相關問題。

72. 何謂「95%」的信賴區間？

73. 對於政黨退出三台有何看法？（財政所）

74. 你對於傳統產業免稅的看法。（財政所）

75. 你認為台商西進大陸，應如何課稅？（財政所）

76. 請闡述福利經濟第一及第二定理。（財政所）

77. 對於舊的稅制與限稅措施有何看法？（財政所）

78. 微軟版權相關問題。（財政所）

79. 你對於跨區就讀明星學校，應收取較高學費的看法是？
    （財政所）

80. 你認為應如何對台北市的觀光飯店課稅？（財政所）

81. 你認為公債是否一定會禍延子孫？（財政所）

82. 國民年金與老人年金是否可一併執行？其間有何關聯？
    （財政所）

83. 你對於「中油敦親睦鄰基金」的看法是？（財政所）

84. 你對於 BOT 案的看法是？（財政所）

85. 你認為國家建設能否以發行公債來因應，為什麼？（財政所）

86. 現在政府財政困窘，以你的觀點來看，國民年金是否應實行？
    為什麼？（財政所）

87. 「立法委員人數減半」及「單一選區兩票制」是否應該實施？
    你的看法為何？（財政所）

88. 關於「統籌分配稅款」，你覺得地方政府是否應該掌握地方財
    政自主權？（財政所）

89. 統籌分配稅款應屬中央或是地方？（財政所）

90. 你認為當初是否應該推行六年國建？（財政所）

第3部份　相關注意事項

1.【目標】中央財管所
　【注意】

　　答題有時間限制（一分鐘），故回答內容須有條理地提出自己的看法。

2.【目標】中山財管所
　【注意】

　　除了採用一般的閒聊方式之外，還會採用壓迫式問答法，口試老師的語氣可能咄咄逼人，考生可事前多加演練，增加自信，以免臨場表現失常。

3.【目標】北大財政所
　【注意】

　　口試前半個小時，會讓考生閱讀一篇英文報告，口試時再問及相關內容。

第三章　統計研究所

　　統計學以機率為理論基礎，配合電腦與軟體的應用，解析龐大數據中的有用訊息。這些數量化的訊息，在資訊時代中，不但提高了研究品質，更成為各行各業決策時的參考基礎，特別是在政府統計機關、市場調查分析、財務金融、保險業等等，統計學正以科技整合的嶄新面向，運用其高度精算技術，在最新科技與傳統產業中佔有一席之地，其影響可說是無遠弗屆。以下將分別介紹，統計類研究所的英文口試常考試題、中文口試常考試題與相關注意事項：

▌第1部份　英文口試常考試題

※ 考生必須朗讀英文題目，並以英文回答問題。

1. One student's grade is lower than the average grade; does that mean he got a low score? If his grade is higher than the average grade; does that mean he got a better score?
   有一位學生的分數比平均分數低，這是否意味著他的成績不好？假如他的分數比平均高，這是否代表說他的成績比較好？

▌第2部份　中文口試常考試題

1. 簡單的自我介紹。一般而言，一開始教授多半會先請你做簡單（一分鐘）的自我介紹，並根據你介紹的內容與審核的資料做延伸的發問。可能觸及的問題為：你的在校成績、是否曾領過獎學金、是否參與過任何活動或學術性演講。

2. 報考該校研究所的動機與未來研究方向。除了要對自己爲何選擇該科系,以及未來想走的路線瞭若指掌外,對於未來研究的方向,和可能會應用到的學科,也必須有深入的認知與了解。例如,可能會請你比較各種理論的異同,說明各種模型的適用範圍,以及把理論應用在實際問題上,藉此觀察你的處理方式。

3. 口試時,教授手上多半會有你筆試的考卷與分數,所以可能會針對你之前答錯的部分,給予提示後,請你再回答一次。因此,考完筆試之後,一定要趕快訂正檢討一遍,有疑惑的地方,務必在口試之前弄懂,否則在口試中被問到,又不會的話,可能會對甄試結果非常不利。

4. 根據成績單詢問你在校表現特優/喜歡,或特差/不喜歡的科目,並提出問題。如果回答說最喜歡的科目是「機率」的話,教授可能會要求你寫出 Markov 不等式,並說出適用條件,運用 Markov 不等式推出 Chebyshev 不等式,再用 Chebyshev 推出弱大數法則,最後再請你求出 MP-TEST。

5. 請你說出一個你在統計上最熟悉的定理,詳述該定理的內容,並舉例說明之。

6. 你大學期間曾經做過哪些調查?做這些調查時如何計算抽樣誤差?曾做過哪些統計領域的報告?內容是什麼?

7. 相關與獨立間關係的應用。

8. 判定一組資料是否符合常態的方法。

9. 常態機率圖的原理,爲何會形成一直線?

10. 迴歸問題及其應用。

11. 迴歸與實設的模型差異何在?

12. 隱函數的證明。

13. 微分法的證明。

14. 請說明如何評估一個估計量的好壞？

15. 提供兩個估計量，考生須在黑板上證明這兩個估計量符合哪些優良性質。

16. 何謂參數？

17. 何謂統計量？

18. 何謂隨機變數（random variable）？

19. 何謂充分統計量？

20. 何謂型一誤差？

21. 何謂極限存在？

22. 何謂連續、可微、微積分定理？

23. 何謂機率公理統計量？

24. cdf 的特性？

25. 何謂中央極限定理？

26. 何謂弱大數法則？何謂強大數法則？有何差異？

27. 何謂泰勒定理？其用途為何？牛頓近似解的步驟。

28. 請說明指數分配、Poisson 分配、幾何分配、二項分配的關係。

29. 解釋信賴區間的意義，及其相關問題。

30. 請問 MLE 與 1-信賴區間為何？

31. 線性代數問題。例如：eigenvalue、eigenvector、對角化矩陣、trace 等相關應用問題。

32. 統計/抽樣問題。例如：

    ⑴ 有 100 名學生平均身高 95%CI 為（110,140），則平均身高落在此區間的機率是否真為 0.95？0.95 的機率與 95%的信心有何差異？若其中有 10 個人不回答，則要如何處置？

⑵ 在 95%信賴水準，誤差 0.03 的要求下要抽多少的 n？若要保守估計，又要抽多少的 n？

⑶ 如果你抽 1067 個樣本，只有 800 筆樣本有效，你該如何處理？

⑷ 假設 2100 萬人中，有 10 萬人患有愛滋病，現在隨機抽取 100 人，請問其中 10 人患有愛滋病的機率是多少？要用何種方式計算？

33. 請寫出母體平均數的假設檢定（單尾或雙尾）。請用母體平均數的信賴區間來檢定前述的假設。

34. 間斷的 LR Test。

35. 作假設檢定及區間估計，並說明假設檢定與區間估計的關係。

36. 找出充分統計量。

37. 機率分配轉換的推導。

38. 機率收斂相關之應用。

39. 算數平均數與中位數及其相關應用。例如：

⑴ 在什麼情況下，哪個比較適合？

⑵ 一般而言，身高與體重成正相關。現在假如有一個又高又瘦與一個又矮又胖的人，請問這兩人是否違反前項敘述？

⑶ 請問如何說明騎機車戴安全帽比不戴安全？

40. 五個槍手打靶，有十顆子彈，要如何選出選手？

41. 給你一張兩位總統候選人的民意調查表，然後請你就這張表，利用你所學的，儘量解釋這張調查表，越多越好。

42. 實驗設計問題。

⑴ 何謂 RBD、CRBS？其差異為何？

⑵ 更深入的實驗設計問題。

第3部份 相關注意事項

1. 【目標】中央統計所

   【注意】

   > 口試時分三組進行，每位學生只須參加一組即可。在輪到你口試的十分鐘前，會給你兩份英文口試題目，一份是統計，一份是數學。利用這十分鐘做準備。口試時間約有 10 ～15 分鐘，不須自我介紹，直接在黑板上解題，教授會根據你解題的內容，問一些相關問題。線性代數中，最常考的題目是正交投影矩陣 (Orthogonal Projection Matrix)。

2. 【目標】政大統計所

   【注意】

   > 口試的順序是隨機安排，每個人約十分鐘，現場備有錄音機。有英文試題，考生必須朗讀英文題目，並以英文回答。

第四章 保險類研究所

　　進入二十一世紀至今,不過短短兩三年的時間,卻接二連三發生了許多天災和人禍。經濟和科技上的突飛猛進,除了帶給人們更便利的生活,也同時埋下許多人禍的種子。針對這樣的現象,社會大眾及產業界對於專業化的保險管理及服務的需求激增。保險類研究所能同時為企業界培養「風險經理人」(risk manager),並為保險界培養「保險經理人」(insurance manager)。而保險業是國內發展最快的熱門產業之一,今後其提供風險保障及資金供給的角色,勢必更加突顯,在此潮流之下,投考保險類研究所的人數也逐年增加。以下將列出推甄保險類研究所時,英文口試常考試題、中文口試常考試題,與相關注意事項:

第1部份 英文口試常考試題

Self-introduction 自我介紹

第2部份 中文口試常考試題

1. 自我介紹,將針對基本資料發問。
   (1) 你的優勢
   (2) 最得意的事、最感到挫折的事
   (3) 修習過的相關課程、印象最深刻的科目、在校成績
   (4) 對未來的規劃、未來研究方向
2. 如果其他學校也獲錄取,你會如何選擇?
3. 報考動機?並會問及其與研究計畫書的關係?
4. 簡述研究計畫的內容。

5. 請以一句話來定義 Hedge。

6. 針對所繳交的報告及參考資料提問。

7. 有哪些國家的長期照護制度可做為我國學習的對象？其採行的政策為何？

8. 提出你對實施長期照護政策的看法與建議。

9. 試描述目前我國長期照護的供需狀態。

10. 倘若實施長期照護保險，相關機構的措施分別為何？

11. 何謂年金屋？

12. 你最欣賞 MSA 哪個委員所提出的法案？為什麼？

13. MSA 中如何判定其適足性？

14. 如何強調 MSA 的現金功能？

15. 社會保險的正義性與 MSA 的現金性如何達成平衡？

16. 現行的全民健保制度有何問題？

17. 請問經濟將市場分成哪幾種？保險在台灣屬於哪一種市場？

18. 何謂共變異數？共變異數和獨立有沒有關係？

19. 利率和保險公司有何關係？

20. 市場蕭條和利率有何關係？

21. 何謂效率市場？

22. 保險公司利用哪些比率調整資產與負債的比例？

23. 對金融控股公司有何看法？（高科大）

24. 逆傳導神經系統與一般統計系統有何不同？（高科大）

25. 何謂死力？何謂息力？（高科大）

26. 死力與死亡機率有何不同？（高科大）

第3部份 相關注意事項

1. 【目標】淡大保險所

   【注意】

   　口試老師會要求考生主動提問，考生應事先準備幾個問題，
   以展現自己的就讀意願。

第五章　會計研究所

　　「會計是商業的語言」這是國外流傳已久的一句話,它印證了會計長久以來對經濟社會的貢獻。會計研究所堪稱商研所之中,實用性最高的研究所。其出路甚為廣泛,除了進入專業會計事務所之外,無論大小公私企業都需要會計人才。在台灣的就業市場上,學會計出身的人就像是捧著鐵飯碗,到哪裡都不用擔心失業。有志考取證照者,更會充分利用兩年的學生生活,善加規劃,然後在畢業後一兩年內取得專業會計師執照。為了幫助讀者順利跨入會計的領域,以下將分別介紹,會計研究所的英文口試常考試題、中文口試常考試題與相關注意事項:

■ 第1部份　英文口試常考試題

　　自我介紹,將針對基本資料發問。

■ 第2部份　中文口試常考試題

　1. 自我介紹
　　(1) 過去修習的課程,你對哪一門課印象最深刻?為什麼?針對大學成績提問、大學的修課狀況、對專業科目的了解程度有多深入?
　　(2) 優缺點?具備什麼優勢進入會研所?是否繼續攻讀博士學位?
　　(3) 參加的社團性質?擔任何種職務?課餘活動為何?
　　(4) 最近看了什麼課外書?看哪一類的雜誌?內容為何?
　　(5) 有無崇拜的偶像?印象最深刻的挫折經驗?
　　(6) 生涯規劃。
　2. 報考研究所的動機?一共報考幾所學校?

3. 以總分為一百分來計算，請替自己在學業、社團、和打工這三方面的表現打個分數。

4. 何謂會計？

5. 如果這個世界上沒有會計會變成什麼樣子？請分別由個體及總體面來回答。

6. 近來會計飽受批評，認為其無法反映新興科技公司的真實價值，甚至還停留在保守的帳面價值，你對這些批評有何看法？

7. 電腦化的企業環境對審計有何影響？

8. 在會計領域中，最喜歡的部分為何？

9. 就你所知，舉例說明最近修改的會計法規。

10. 對寫程式是否有興趣？（中正會研）

11. 研發費用為何不能當作資產？

12. 唸研究所對生涯規劃有何幫助？

13. 如果與教授發生衝突，你將如何處理？

14. 無形資產是否應該入帳，為什麼？

15. 在財務會計準則公報中，挑一號公報解釋說明。

16. 你覺得人際關係重要還是工作能力重要？

第3部份 相關注意事項

1.【目標】台大會研所
  【注意】
   會考英文文章閱讀，讀完之後須以英文說出大意。

2. 【目標】政大會研所
　　【注意】

　　　(1) 有三分鐘的即席演講，題目多跟會計師的職業、時事剖
　　　　析相關，如下：
　　　　① 給定幾個城市，問學生願意選擇哪個地方執業？
　　　　② 如果老闆在上班時間要求你幫他處理私人事務，你
　　　　　會怎麼做？
　　　　③ 假如你是素食主義者，當和上司或長輩同桌吃飯時，
　　　　　卻忽然發現滿桌只有葷菜，請問你會如何處置？
　　　　④ 你認為台灣的產業未來該何去何從？
　　　　⑤ 你對貴校選課系統的看法。
　　　　⑥ 你最喜歡的一本書。
　　　　⑦ 關於審計方面的專業題目。

　　　(2) 考前應多閱讀經濟日報、工商時報和商業周刊，針對熱
　　　　門議題要記下重點，並練習發表自己的意見或加以剖析。
　　　　口試時若被問及不熟悉的領域，也毋須太過緊張，只要
　　　　以有條理的方式說出自己的看法。政大教授十分注重考
　　　　生的臨場反應。

　　　(3) 若相關資料顯示，該名考生的語言能力不錯，則可能被
　　　　要求以英語回答。

第六章　經濟類研究所

經濟類研究所畢業生的就業市場以金融相關產業（包括金控公司、銀行、證券、保險等行業）、一般公司行號、公職為主。若不投入就業市場者，則通常會選擇繼續深造或從事學術研究。無論就業或深造，學經濟出身者，在各行各業間分佈的深度和廣度，可以證明其生涯發展將有無限寬廣的空間。此外，台灣過去三十幾年的經濟發展，締造了全球矚目的經濟奇蹟，而今正值國內經濟發展的轉捩點，於邁向國際舞台之際，經濟類研究所將是二十一世紀的主角之一。以下將列出推甄經濟類研究所時，英文口試常考試題、中文口試常考試題，與相關注意事項：

▌第 1 部份　英文口試常考試題

1. Self-introduction　自我介紹
2. Job Description in English　請描述你的工作。
3. Where's your college?　你的學校在哪裡？
4. Why do you choose this university?　為何選考本校？
5. What will you do after you get an MBA?
   拿到 MBA 之後想做什麼？

▌第 2 部份　中文口試常考試題

1. 中文自我介紹，會針對相關基本資料提問。（例如：報考動機、求學過程、影響你最深的人）
2. 何時開始準備筆試？
3. 為何想唸經研所？
4. 家住哪裡？有沒有看考古題？有沒有補習？

5. 對本所筆試題目的看法。

6. 如果給自己打分數，你認為自己在研究所考試可以拿幾分？

7. 未來預定主修與志向。

8. 研究計劃的寫作動機和詳細內容。

9. 研究生應有的做學問態度為何？

10. 進入研究所後，要用何種方法來作研究？

11. 學校的計量課程教到哪裡？用哪一本課本？

12. 大學修過哪些專業科目？成績如何？覺得自己是否有盡力？

13. 最欣賞哪一位經濟學家，為什麼？

14. 對於非單一選票制度的看法。

15. 對於立委薪俸減半的看法。

16. 是否支持舉債式的財政政策，為什麼？

17. 健保虧損累累，是否應該繼續經營？請提出你對健保改革的看法。

18. 失業保險應如何避免重蹈健保覆轍，你認為失業保險是否應該開辦與如何經營？

19. 台灣有哪些產業需要政府管制？請舉例。

20. 對於有線新聞業者採聯合採訪的看法。

21. 是否應管制固網產業？

22. 請問重貨幣學派和凱因斯學派在貨幣政策上有何不同的看法？

23. 何謂貨幣需求函數？函數中的利率及所得為實質或名目的？若不穩定時，在圖形中要如何表達？

24. 試用國際金融的理論來分析歐元的走向。

25. 何謂產業間貿易？

26. 在什麼情形下增加貨幣供給，會使利率上升？

27. 請問傳統預期理論和理性預期理論有何不同？

28. 赤字財政可行嗎？何謂混合政策？

29. 何謂拉式乘數？

30. 為何檢定時要用 t 檢定而不用 z 檢定？

31. 什麼是「Rule o 72」？

32. 如何在兩個消費物品與所得限制內使效用最大？寫出前提、數學式與圖形。

33. 限制所得的因子有哪些？請寫出數學式並畫出圖形。

34. 政府是否應管制資金的流動？

35. 何謂不偏性、一致性？

36. 何謂衡量誤差，如果有衡量誤差該如何解決？

37. 對行政院所推出的 8100 億擴大內需方案的看法。

38. 請解釋何謂效率？

39. 何謂市場均衡及外部性？

40. 何謂多工廠獨占？其與差別取價之相異處為何？

41. 影響貨幣需求的因素為何？

42. 中央銀行降息對貨幣需求的影響為何？

43. 菲利浦曲線是否會為正斜率，其原因為何？

44. 若菲利浦曲線為正斜率，AS 線是否會為負斜率，其原因為何？

45. 哪些因素會影響利率？

46. 為什麼如果美國降息，台灣也會跟著降息呢？

47. 試由總體經濟的觀點，描述台灣目前的經濟現況。

48. 不偏性、有效性及統計量的定義。

49. 在做估計時平均數與中位數何者較佳？

50. 何謂函數關係（試解釋 $y = f(x)$），可以一對多或多對一嗎？

51. 何謂凹函數與凸函數？

52. 如何利用一階微分與二階微分求極大、極小值？

53. 如果有一組資料，你要如何衡量其中心趨勢？

54. 求解效用最大化的問題。

55. 「給我手機，其餘免談！」請描述其效用函數。

56. 何謂統計量？若要估計 μ 時，算術平均數和中位數何者較佳？為什麼？

57. 對於 μ 而言，何謂好的估計量？

58. 若在無限制條件下求效用極大，其一階及二階條件為何？在有限制條件之下求效用極大，一階及二階條件又為何？若不使用二階條件，要如何判斷求出的 X、Y 最適解是否符合效用極大？

59. 台灣經濟衰退的原因？

60. 加入 WTO 對台灣經濟有何影響？

61. 若政府採取金錢補助或職業訓練，你的選擇為何？為什麼？

62. 央行降息可以刺激什麼？如果不降息，則資金流向為何？

63. 根據凱因斯的 IS-LM 模型，貨幣政策在何種狀況下最有效？

64. 貨幣政策對產出影響的傳導機制。

65. 針對美國的景氣衰退，你認為應該採取財政政策或是貨幣政策？為什麼？

66. 何謂 Pareto 效率條件及公平的定義？

67. 市場失靈的種類有哪些？

68. 如何解決逆選擇的問題？

69. 何謂信賴區間？影響檢定結果的因素爲何？

70. 何謂型一誤差、型二誤差？

71. 差別取價與需求彈性方面的問題。

72. 對台商赴大陸投資的看法。

73. 對台灣景氣的未來是抱持樂觀或悲觀的看法，爲什麼？

74. 何謂囚犯兩難？

75. 請說明 Bertrand model、Cournot model 的定義與其競爭均衡結果。

76. 對米酒事件的看法與需求彈性的問題，如替代品增加需求彈性的變化。威士忌與米酒，哪一個的需求彈性較大？

77. 何謂消費者行爲與時間偏好率？

78. 台灣早期有哪些自然獨占的產業？自然獨占的成因爲何？應如何解決？

79. 何謂一級、二級、三級差別取價？其與社會總剩餘的變化關係爲何？

80. 何謂 Nash 均衡與 Pareto 效率？兩者的關係爲何？

81. 如何導出需求曲線？

82. 如何判斷風險態度（風險愛好者、趨避者或是中立者）？

83. 何謂變異數異質性等問題。

84. 變異數與標準差。

85. 存貨週轉率、R^2 的定義。

86. 流動資產與速動資產的相異之處。

87. Mega Marketing 的定義。

88. Consumer 與 Customer 的不同點。

89. 美國對於京都議定書的態度爲何？（農經所）

90. 在環境、資源方面，Coase 定理是屬於技術面的方法，那你知道關於哲學方面的學派嗎？（農經所）

91. 農業政策的形成過程及方式爲何？（農經所）

92. 如果你是農委會主委，面對立委的脅迫，你會妥協嗎？（農經所）

93. 對此面試有何問題？

94. 你對大學聯盟的看法爲何？

95. 你對晶圓廠外移的看法爲何？

▌第 3 部份　相關注意事項

1.【目標】中央產經所
　【注意】
　　⑴ 該所考題較偏向個體經濟學。口試前會要求考生先填一份問卷，須謹慎作答，口試老師會依據該問卷出題。
　　⑵ 考前十分鐘會先抽口試題目，故考生的準備時間還算充裕，無須太過緊張。口試時如果有任何疑問或聽不懂的地方，可以請老師說明或提示，避免自己隨便回答。

2.【目標】政大經濟所
　【注意】
　　⑴ 該所考題偏向總體經濟學，會考時事分析。可能會指定某個理論，請考生做個案分析。
　　⑵ 會針對考生所提的研究計劃或書面報告提問，故考生要事前做好完善的準備。

第七章　資管資工研究所

　　科技發展是評估國家總體競爭力的重要考量之一，而資訊科技又是我國近幾年高度發展的科技項目之一。最近，以資訊電子為主的資訊工業已逐漸取代傳統產業，除了主導台灣的經濟動向之外，也在世界舞台上扮演著引人注目的角色。相信再過幾年，台灣的資訊軟體與服務業將成為最重要的產業。說到推動資訊工業發展，最重要的因素，莫過於專業人才的培育，而這項任務的達成，需要依賴專業的研究所教育。針對有志報考資管、或資工類研究所的考生，以下將分別介紹，英文口試常考試題、中文口試常考試題與相關注意事項：

第1部份　英文口試常考試題

1. Describe your college life.　What's your favorite subject in college?　What's your worst subject in college?
   請描述你的大學生活。你大學時最喜歡哪個科目？你大學時最糟的科目是什麼？

2. Please recommend a movie which is about information technology.　請推薦一部和資訊科技有關的電影。

3. What do you want to do after you get into this school?
   進研究所後，想做些什麼？

4. What's the most memorable thing that happened in your college life?　大學生活中，最難忘的事是什麼？

5. What will you do after you graduate from this school?
   你畢業之後要做什麼？

6. What is the most impressive book you've read?
   你讀過印象最深刻的一本書是什麼？

▌第2部份 中文口試常考試題

1. 自我介紹。（會問及在校成績、讀書方法、生涯規劃）

2. 你修過的課程中，哪一科讓你印象最深刻？你從這門科目所學到的知識對系統開發有何用處？如何應用？

3. 你最喜歡與最不喜歡的科目為何？為什麼某科分數偏低？

4. 大學時最喜愛的三個科目為何？（會從回答內容再衍伸出題）

5. 是否曾參與任何課外活動或打工？

6. 你曾做過哪些系統？試說明之。

7. 就考生參與過的專案提問。

8. 你的英文能力如何？

9. 報考動機？

10. 專題的題目與內容為何？（使用了哪些演算法或數學？專題是否獨立完成？如果是小組合作的話，你負責的部分為何？）

11. 未來研究方向。

12. 未來想升學還是就業？如果是就業，你想自己創業還是到大型科技公司的資訊部門工作？

13. 如果你的生命只剩一天，你會做些什麼？

14. 解釋何謂 Data mining？

15. 解釋何謂 E-R diagram？

16. 解釋資料庫正規化的五步驟為何？

17. 資料結構中 Tree 的種類有哪些？其應用為何？

18. 在資管領域中，大學、研究所的區別為何？

19. ERP 和 EC 的關係？

20. 對行動通訊的看法。

21. 如何解決軟體危機？

22. 對出國參加電玩比賽拿冠軍的少年曾政承，有何看法？

23. 請描述 array, link list, tree 的相同與相異處。

24. 機智問答：有三個人（甲、乙、丙）去住宿，房租 30 元，於是每人拿 10 元，湊成 30 元後，派甲將 30 元交給房東。房東說房租費 25 元即可，便退還甲 5 元，由於 5 元無法均分給 3 個人，於是甲便將 2 元拿去捐給慈善機構，剩餘 3 元每人分 1 元。於是三人事後回想，每人出 9 元：$9 \times 3 = 27$ 元，另外加上 2 元捐款：$27 + 2 = 29$，然而當初明明是拿 30 元給房東，請問 1 塊錢跑哪去了？（回答時間：2 分鐘）

25. Microsoft 程式設計師及系統分析師的差異。

26. 如何運用資訊系統，在資訊不充分的情況下，幫雇主做出正確的決定？

27. 你個人認為資訊技術運用在哪個行業，可以發揮最大的效能？

28. 目前最熱門的資訊議題為何？

29. 資管系的程式會比企管系強嗎？

30. 網站式的系統在考量備用系統上要注意哪些因素？

31. 請簡述系統發展的未來趨勢。

32. 請區分 C++ 與 Java 的異同。

33. 資料庫中 index 和 key 的差別為何？

34. 你對資訊管理的認識。

35. 作業系統 process 和 thread 的 IPC 有何不同？

36. 在「計算機組織」這門課程中學到些什麼？

37. 試敘述 Compiler 的過程。

38. 試述中斷的程序。

▌第 3 部份 ▶ 相關注意事項

1.【目標】中央資管所
   【注意】

   口試前會先考英文筆試，類似 GMAT，故考生可事先做相關準備。

2.【目標】中山資管所
   【注意】

   面試分兩關，其中第二關會要求現場閱讀兩篇報告，一篇中文，一篇英文，然後再根據報告內容提問，建議在口試前多練習閱讀英文報告。

3.【目標】淡大資管所
   【注意】

   該所無資格審查，故面試人數特別多，每個人分配的時間極短，考生務必對自己的研究計劃相關領域十分熟悉，才能以最簡短有力的方式回答口試老師的問題。

4.【目標】台大資工所
   【注意】

   (1) 口試問題可能與該名教授的專長領域相關，考生可先上該所的網站，至少可對教授有初步認識，對口試會有一定程度的幫助。
   (2) 會針對考生畢業專題發問，故口試前要有完善的準備。

第八章　工業類研究所

　　台灣科技產業在最近幾年突飛猛進，一下子躍升為國際科技舞台上的佼佼者，工業管理的角色也從過去默默無名的員工，演變成「系統的整合者」，其工作的場所不再侷限於製造工廠內。因此無論在各校學程的安排，或國科會針對學門、服務系統、資訊系統，以及人機系統相關的教學與研究規劃，工業管理儼然已成為未來的主流發展。為了成為自動化科學管理，和系統整合能力的高級工業管理人才，進而提高產業品質、促進工業升級及追求最大經濟效益，目前投考工業類研究所也是許多人的目標之一，相關的研究所包括工業工程所、工業管理所和工業資管所。以下將列出推甄工業類研究所時，中文口試常考試題，與相關注意事項：

■ 第1部份　中文口試常考試題

1. 自我介紹兩分鐘。
    (1) 詢問與大學成績有關問題，如：某科成績為何不好等。詢問在校成績排名，為何大一、大二成績不佳？為什麼大學多唸一年？你在系上的排名為何？
    (2) 是否有補習？
    (3) 提出一些讓老師錄取你的理由。
    (4) 優缺點為何？有何專長？（會根據回答延伸發問，你知道本所哪位老師對這方面有研究？）
    (5) 試述中長期的人生規畫。

2. 為何不等畢業再來考呢？

3. 報考動機。

4. 你認為你要學的東西一定要到研究所才能學得到嗎？

5. 爲何從所學的領域轉向工管？

6. 除了本校，還報考了哪些學校？將如何選擇？

7. 未來研究方向？

8. 爲何不準備人因工程，是不是這科比較好考？

9. 你覺得今年的考題出得如何？

10. 爲何想考工管所？

11. 大學並無修習相關工管課程，將來如何研讀本所課程？

12. 詢問初試的成績，並評論自己哪些科目考得好或不好，爲什麼？

13. 閒談大學生活概況。

14. 是否爲應屆畢業生？如不是，則詢問從去年到今年的讀書計畫？

15. （針對非本系生）你認爲你唸工業管理的相對優勢是什麼？若能進入本所，你的研究方向爲何？

16. 你修過「統計與人生」，請問統計與人生的關係爲何，又人生與迴歸是否有相關？

17. 工作經驗中有哪些應用到工業工程或管理？工作心得？

18. 非本科系學生，將來要補修學分，是否有問題？

19. 曾修過哪種程式語言？

20. 對工管的瞭解爲何？

21. 何謂作業研究？

22. 何謂管理數學？教授的內容爲何？

23. 何謂卡方分配？

24. 在校曾修過哪些程式語言？

25. 如果指導教授要你一年畢業,你將如何規劃這一年?

26. 最佳化技術有哪些?

27. 是否修過研究作業?

28. 針對大學歷年所修習的科目,詢問該方面的專業問題以及課程內容。

29. 爲何選考工業工程而不考其他類的研究所?

30. 爲什麼要自動化?其重要性爲何?

31. 工業自動化的範圍爲何?

32. 你曾經參觀過某某科技公司,可否介紹一下該公司的特色。

33. 請說明根據這家公司的特性,應該採取何種生產制度或方式?

34. 你認爲它應該採用 JIT 生產,還是 MRP 或 MRPII?

35. 請問何謂科技管理?

36. 請解釋一下什麼是 ARIS?

37. 你認爲產業升級和園區管理有無關係,爲什麼?

38. 產業外移對本土工業區的影響爲何?

■ 第 2 部份　相關注意事項

1. 【目標】台大工業工程所
   【注意】
   會針對成績單和所繳交的報告資料提問。對於非本科系學生,則幾乎不問工業工程的專業問題。

2. 【目標】清大工業工程所
   【注意】
   口試時,教授多半針對學生所學的領域提問,不太會問工業工程的專業問題。

3. 【目標】交通大學工業工程所

【注意】

(1) 口試時，會要求以投影片自我介紹。

(2) 口試進行中，該所非常注重時間控制，故考生回答問題要特別注意時間限制。

心得筆記欄

$E = mc^2$

新一代英語教科書・領先全世界

學習語言以口說為主・是全世界的趨勢

劉毅 TOEIC 700 分保證班

> ✓ 一次繳費，終生上課
> ✓ 學費全國最低
> ✓ 獨家研發教材（非賣品）
> ✓ 一次繳費，所有多益班皆可上課

1. 問：什麼是「TOEIC 700 分保證」？

答：凡是報名保證班的同學，我們保證你考取 700 分。如果未達到 700 分，就可以免費一直上課，考上 700 分為止，不再另外收費，但是你必須每年至少考一次 TOEIC 測驗，考不到 700 分，可憑成績單，繼續上課，考上 700 分為止。

2. 問：你們用什麼教材？

答：我們請資深美籍老師，根據 TOEIC 最新出題來源改編，全新試題，市面上沒有，但是考試必有雷同出現。

3. 問：「TOEIC 700 分保證班」如何收費？

答：「TOEIC 700 分保證班」終生無限上課，僅收 19,800 元。一次繳費，所有多益班皆可上課。

4. 問：你們有什麼贈書？

答：報名後贈送「TOEIC MODEL TEST ①～④」及聽力原文、「TOEIC 聽力測驗講義」、「TOEIC 口說測驗講義」、「TOEIC 必考字彙」、「TOEIC 文法 700 題」、「TOEIC 字彙 500 題」、「TOEIC 聽力測驗」。我們全力協助同學應試，只要有關「多益」的書籍，通通贈送給你。

5. 上課時間：

	班　　級	上　課　時　間	收　費　標　準
台北	TOEIC 台北 A 班	每週一晚上 7:00～9:00	*19,800* 元
	TOEIC 台北 B 班	每週日晚上 7:00～9:00	（可選一班，也可同時上兩班）
	TOEIC 台北寫作班	每週三晚上 7:00～9:00 外師免費不限次數批改	*9,900* 元（報名多益班即贈送口說班）
	TOEIC 台北口說班	不限次數約定小班上課	*9,900* 元（報名多益班即贈送口說班）
台中	TOEIC 台中班	每週六下午 2:00～5:00	*19,800* 元
	TOEIC 台中口說班	不限次數約定小班上課	*9,900* 元（報名多益班即贈送口說班）

※ 以上課表會依實際上課情形調整。

6. 問：在哪裡報名上課？

答：台北市許昌街 17 號 6F（壽德大樓）（劉毅英文家教班高中部）☎ (02) 2389-5212
台中市三民路三段 125 號 7F（太平路口，加州健身中心樓上）☎ (04) 2221-8861

面談英語

修　　　編 / 王淑平

發　行　所 / 學習出版有限公司　　　☎ (02) 2704-5525

郵 撥 帳 號 / 0512727-2 學習出版社帳戶

登　記　證 / 局版台業 2179 號

印　刷　所 / 裕強彩色印刷有限公司

台 北 門 市 / 台北市許昌街 10 號 2 F　　☎ (02) 2331-4060・2331-9209

台灣總經銷 / 紅螞蟻圖書有限公司　　　☎ (02) 2795-3656

美國總經銷 / Evergreen Book Store　　☎ (818) 2813622

本公司網址　www.learnbook.com.tw

電子郵件　learnbook@learnbook.com.tw

售價：新台幣二百八十元正

2009 年 1 月 1 日新修訂